Norman Loc

"A mesmerizingly twisted, richly layered homage to a pioneer of American Gothic fiction."
—*New York Times Book Review* on *The Port-Wine Stain*

"[Walt Whitman] hovers over [*American Meteor*], just as Mark Twain's spirit pervaded *The Boy in His Winter*. . . . Like all Mr. Lock's books, this is an ambitious work, where ideas crowd together on the page like desperate men on a battlefield."
—*Wall Street Journal* on *American Meteor*

"Sheds brilliant light along the meteoric path of American westward expansion. . . . [A] pithy, compact beautifully conducted version of the American Dream."—**NPR** on *American Meteor*

"Make[s] Huck and Jim so real you expect to get messages from them on your iPhone."
—**NPR** *Weekend Edition* on *The Boy in His Winter*

"Lock writes some of the most deceptively beautiful sentences in contemporary fiction. Beneath their clarity are layers of cultural and literary references, profound questions about loyalty, race, the possibility of social progress, and the nature of truth. They merge with an iconic American character, tall tales intact, to create something entirely new— an American fable of ideas."—*Shelf Awareness* on *The Boy in His Winter*

"[Lock] is one of the most interesting writers out there."
—*Reader's Digest*

"One could spend forever worming through [Lock's] magicked words, their worlds."—*The Believer*

"[Lock's writing] lives up to Whitman's words . . . no other writer, in recent memory, dares the reader to believe there is a hand reaching out to be held, a hand to hold onto us."
—**Detroit** *Metro Times*

"Lock is a rapturous storyteller, and his tales are never less than engrossing."—*Kenyon Review*

"One of our country's unsung treasures."
—*Green Mountains Review*

"Our finest modern fabulist." —*Bookslut*

"A master of the unusual." —*Slice* **magazine**

"A master storyteller." —*Largehearted Boy*

"[A] contemporary master of the form [and] virtuosic fabulist." —*Flavorwire*

"[Lock's] window onto fiction [is] a welcome one: at once referential and playful, occupying a similar post-Borges space to . . . Stephen Millhauser and Neil Gaiman." —*Vol. 1 Brooklyn*

"[Lock] is not engaged in either homage or pastiche but in an intense dialogue with a number of past writers about the process of writing, and the nature of fiction itself." —*Weird Fiction*

"Lock's work mines the stuff of dreams." —*Rumpus*

"You can feel the joy leaping off the page." —*Full Stop*

"Lock plays profound tricks, with language—his is crystalline and underline-worthy." —*Publishers Weekly*

"[Lock] writes beautifully, with many subtle, complex insights." —*Booklist*

"[Lock] successfully blends beautiful language reminiscent of 19th-century prose with cynicism and bald, ugly truth."
—*Library Journal*

"Lock's stories stir time as though it were a soup . . . beyond the entertainment lie 21st-century conundrums: What really exists? Are we each, ultimately, alone and lonely? Where is technology taking humankind?" —*Kirkus Reviews*

"All hail Lock, whose narrative soul sings fairy tales, whose language is glass."
—**Kate Bernheimer**, editor of *xo Orpheus: Fifty New Myths, My Mother She Killed Me, My Father He Ate Me,* and *Fairy Tale Review*

"[Lock] has an impressive ability to create a unique and original world."
—**Brian Evenson**, author of *Immobility* and *A Collapse of Horses*

"Lock is one of our great miniaturists, to be read only a single time at one's peril." —**Tim Horvath**, author of *Understories*

"A writer exquisite in the singularity (read for this 'genius') of his utterance." —**Gordon Lish**

—*A*—
FUGITIVE
in
WALDEN WOODS

—*A*—
FUGITIVE
in
WALDEN WOODS

Norman Lock

Bellevue Literary Press
New York

First published in the United States in 2017 by
Bellevue Literary Press, New York

For information, contact:
Bellevue Literary Press
NYU School of Medicine
550 First Avenue
OBV A612
New York, NY 10016

Library of Congress Cataloging-in-Publication Data
is available from the publisher upon request

Bellevue Literary Press would like to thank all its generous
donors—individuals and foundations—for their support.

This publication is made possible by the New York
State Council on the Arts with the support of Governor
Andrew Cuomo and the New York State Legislature.

This project is supported in part
by an award from the National
Endowment for the Arts.

Book design and composition by Mulberry Tree Press, Inc.

Manufactured in the United States of America
First Edition

1 3 5 7 9 8 6 4 2

paperback ISBN: 978-1-942658-22-1

ebook ISBN: 978-1-942658-23-8

For E.G.

I should not talk so much about myself if there were anybody else I knew as well.

—Henry David Thoreau

There is no history. There is only biography.

—Ralph Waldo Emerson

— $\mathcal{A}$ —
FUGITIVE
in
WALDEN WOODS

(Summer 1845–Fall 1846)

Begun on May 11, 1862, by Samuel Long, Freedman,
in Memory of Henry Thoreau,
Who Died on May 6 of That Year;
Finished in Philadelphia on December 20, 1862.

I

I HAVE ALWAYS MAINTAINED THAT, in his bean rows, Henry Thoreau revealed his true character. There one could see the exactitude of the mechanic and land surveyor at variance with the fancies of the loafer and philosopher. Henry combined both strands of human nature in his makeup; it was this mixture that made him contrarious. His bean rows, as I pointed out to him on more than one occasion, were three parts agriculture, one part invention. Had he been born and raised, like me, in slavery, he would have given his master the very great happiness of beating him to within an inch of his life. It takes but a single lash more than what the welted flesh can bear to deliver the body across that inch into extinction, which some have reason to call blessed. A free man, Henry could let his rows wander with his thoughts, if he had a mind to do so. His mind, as we know, was often elsewhere, while, even after my escape to the North, mine—a part of it anyway—strained like a plow horse to evade the driver's scourge. I strove always to ingratiate myself, as would anyone or anything whose existence depended on the good opinion of others.

I first set eyes on Henry Thoreau in the summer of 1845, in the little woods owned by Ralph Waldo Emerson near Concord. I had been a fugitive since '44, when I disenthralled myself from the stable where my master had had me shackled next to his most valuable Thoroughbred, Bucephalus, in order to teach me to respect the rights of property and of southern horseflesh. It took zeal, resolve, an ax, and a bucket of pine tar to free myself—the ax and tar, used to dress the horses' hooves, belonged to my master, Mr. Jeroboam, but the zeal and resolution mustered to chop off my hand and dip the bloody stump into hot tar were all my own. Fortunately for me, I was fastened to Bucephalus's stall by just a single manacle—Jeroboam called it a "coon cuff." While I was desperate to be gone, I would not have had the courage to chop off both my hands.

Unless you have been scourged with a "cat" or thrashed as if you were nothing but a heap of wheat, the pain of amputation is unimaginable. It would be indelicate of me and offensive to the ladies to liken it to childbearing, which the Bible calls "travail" to give it its due. I would have screamed—and most likely bitten off my tongue like a chaw of tobacco—if it had not been for the iron bit in my mouth, put there by my overseer to remind me of my status, which was much lower than the horse's. If it had not been for the tar that cauterized the wound, I would have crossed over

Jordan into "nigger heaven," which is what unkind folks call our promised land of broken-down cribs and juke joints, with a minstrel show on Saturday night and a fish fry on the Sabbath to keep us "darkies" happy.

I admit that, in my frenzy, I nearly massacred the horse with the ax I had used to correct the accident of birth that had caused me to be born into slavery. But for all his fancy airs and graces, Bucephalus was no more at fault than I, and, though he was a prizewinning quarter horse and a stud to boot, he had even less liberty than most colored people. I had infuriated Mr. Jeroboam, which, of course, is not his real name. I have acquaintances in Virginia, left behind when I escaped with my life and nothing else, and would not want them to suffer on account of my frankness. Jeroboam locked me in the stable because I had allowed a stone to get stuck in a hoof, which might have lamed Bucephalus and prevented him from racing Horace Merriman's stallion Meteor at the National Course, in Washington City. The five-thousand-dollar purse was ten times what Jeroboam had paid for me, a black child who had been taught his table manners and his alphabet by an old harridan belonging to one of Richmond's genteel families. My color is that of the horse chestnut, which Mistress S— thought highly desirable in a house nigger. She admired my "coat" as much as Jeroboam did Bucephalus's, which it resembled in color and gloss. Why a Christian gentleman saw fit to spoil my hide with the whip and not that of his horse, which could be as recalcitrant as any of his human property, testifies to the horse's superior breeding. Jeroboam could trace Bucephalus's ancestors back five generations, while I did not know so much as the Christian names of my mother and father. I worked harder than a hardscrabble farmer's mule for my master, ate my slops without fussing, and never showed him my teeth or nickered at him. He beat me nonetheless.

So I ran away.

In some states in the Union, I am considered no better than a thief. I had been bought and paid for—"at a fair price!"—by *Massa* Jeroboam. He had my bill of sale to prove it. I was there when he showed it to his daughter—a pretty moppet without a particle of meanness—after he had upset her by bloodying my thick African lips with a heavy gold ring decorating his fist. In spite of his legal right to me, I broke God's eighth commandment jubilantly and stole myself out of bondage. I would also break His sixth with good reason. To tell the truth, which I hope to do, I had become sick to death of the "thou shalt nots"—especially those laid down by the white race exclusively for the black one. In their number and absurdity, they would have astonished Moses on Mount Sinai and—if He were not preoccupied with the glory of His sunsets and the sublimity of His mountains—would vex the Almighty, for whom ten commandments had been a sufficient number to keep mankind in check.

I confess that I did steal myself from my lawful master, Jeroboam, and I have no more to say on the subject.

I have decided to write about a man who figured largely in the story of my life and to add my grief to the general sorrow that has welled up out of New England's soil—product of a nature too flinty and miserly to be called bucolic. This book of mine—if such it will turn out to be—is a wreath laid on the gravestone of a man who briefly walked among us without much "show" and with no thoughts at all of wealth. At the outset of our—I will call it "friendship" for the sake of simplicity—I had mistaken Henry Thoreau for an ordinary man with all the faults of our kind, when, in actuality, he was an extraordinary one with only a few of them. I shall try to tell how it was for him and for me in Walden Woods after he had gone there to live on Independence Day 1845, until September 1846, when I left them for good.

I had gone into the woods and built a shack of my own before the start of his rustication. I went at the request of his friend Waldo Emerson. It was Emerson who had taken me in after a harrowing escape from my "Egypt," and it was he who would later take up a subscription among the abolitionists to buy me my freedom. When I had first arrived in the village—for me, the last station of the Underground Railroad—I lived under his protection. He began the long, difficult task of illuminating my benighted mind. Thoreau, also, would do much to enlarge my perception of the world. But it would be left for me to finish the task, which is as it should be, although I have yet to do so.

If I had not been a negro slave, I would express my eternal gratitude to Mr. Emerson, Mr. Garrison, Mr. Wendell Phillips, Henry, and to others who redeemed me. But in that I *am* a negro and I *was* a slave, I realize as fully as a man or a woman can the fugitive, uncertain quality of life, which makes notions like freedom and eternity no more than pretty stories with which to console a child during the terrors of the night. What is more, if the reader will pardon me, I insist that I am in debt to no one for restoring what ought to have been mine since birth. The sparrow is not obligated to the rain that quenches its thirst and causes the earth to give up its worms. I am a man. Is a man any less than a bird? What is this impertinence but the self-reliance that Emerson espouses and Thoreau practiced in his lifetime. Like them, I wish to be reliant on no one but myself.

I was no less a man when I was no more than an entry in Jeroboam's ledger book. But the full flowering of a person is impossible under the blight of slavery. Human beings cannot survive the frost of all their hopes. Hamlet's "nutshell" aside, I was no "king of infinite space" in the slave pen, on the auctioneer's block, at the whipping post, or while manacled to a stable wall. There must be more than a constancy of pain, sadness, and fear—heart and spirit must be unbroken—if we are to be anything other than "chattel personal" by law and according to our owners' accounts. Black people are not so many chains, rags, and bales of cotton to be overseen by slave drivers and valuated by bookkeepers.

Now I must tell a terrible truth: There is no nobility in suffering, no wisdom born of pain, no holiness that will suffuse a tortured soul and exalt it. To preach otherwise is to be guilty of sentimentality, as onerous for any despised people as the bigots' calumnies. Ignorance begets ignorance; prejudice breeds enmity; viciousness becomes the common coin of men. We are not purged of our base nature by misery, nor is the gross part of us burned clean by fiery torments. Except for a few saints among us of whatever color, suffering is a rancorous thorn in the heart. Enraged at times past enduring, I could have cut my master's throat, along with his wife's and their innocent daughter's, for there is no restraining a man who has been robbed of his manhood.

Bondage, as Frederick Douglass said, is "the graveyard of the mind." In answer, Wendell Phillips wrote to him: "You began . . . to gauge the wretchedness of the slave, not by his hunger and want, not by his lashes and toil, but by the cruel and blighting death which gathers over his soul." That death is the extinguishment of the small fire given us at birth to warm our hearts and to lighten our spirits during the winter that is in store for every one of us.

Setting out to write, I had no thought of composing a slave narrative. What could I add to the accounts written by Henry Bibb, Moses Roper, Solomon Northup, or Frederick Douglass? Instead, I had intended that this writing should be a eulogy in praise of the great heart and mind that belonged to Henry David Thoreau.

He died on May 6 and was buried in Sleepy Hollow Cemetery, in his native soil. He was let down on ropes into a gash of freshly opened earth, in the family plot, his coffin decked with wildflowers. I think that he would have preferred to lie beneath a tree, where a man or woman might pause long enough to contemplate eternity, which is said to be without end, but can also exist within the brief space of a pain or sorrow. He had "travelled much in Concord" for forty-four years, which, for such a man as he was—a "consumptive" of the body, the spirit, and the senses—was a good age. According to his friend Nathaniel Hawthorne, Henry was "as ugly as sin"—always Hawthorne would harp on sin!—"long-nosed, queer-mouthed, and with uncouth and rustic, though courteous manners, corresponding very well with such an exterior." But his ugliness and rough manners became him, said Hawthorne, as they do Mr. Lincoln, whom the world calls "Honest Abe."

I was not in Concord when Henry died, but for a time, I was with him where he was, perhaps, most alive: in the woods outside Concord. We came to know each other tolerably well; I have yet to understand anyone half so much. In that he loved John Brown and detested slavery, I owe him my regard. Although I did not always bear him affection or show him my goodwill, I have greater cause to care for Henry Thoreau than I can admit. I do not mean to be secretive—nothing annoys so much as a wink and a nod hinting at a mystery. God knows how much relief it would bring me to be rid of it. But for Henry's sake and my own, I must keep the secret until his reputation and my well-being are beyond injuring.

Henry and I spoke together for the first time toward the end of August 1845. He was watching the sun go down above the trees to the west of the clearing where his house stood. To call it a "house" is to do it more justice than it deserved, although it was well made, like his sentences, and, for him who lived in it, comfortable and sufficient to his needs, which were few. It might have been his apparent delight in austerity that annoyed me that evening.

I had entered the clearing warily—not that I had anything to fear from him, but it was, even in Massachusetts, habitual for me to approach a white person with apprehension. At the sound of my approach, he reluctantly turned his gaze from the colorful rags of a summer's dusk.

"Good evening, Mr. Thoreau," I said. "Allow me to introduce myself. My name is—"

"I know who you are, Mr. Long. You are Waldo Emerson's . . ."

What word he might have used to define my relationship to the celebrated man of letters—whether *man, boy, charity,* or *friend*—was left unsaid.

"Yes," I replied, willing at that moment to be called by any name that Henry wished. The habits of the bondman persist long after the chains have been struck off.

"I've noticed your comings and goings," he said gruffly.

Henry was too honest always to be agreeable. Courtiers are ingratiating, but he was a man who did not curry favor. Ministers are polite, but to Henry, religion and government were matters for the individual conscience alone. He had strong principles, but he would not have forced them on anyone. He would never truckle or fawn, nor would he tolerate flattery. He had peeled the veneer of civilization like bark from a stick. Henry was a natural man, as forthright as the sunset he had been admiring. It went about its business without a thought to pleasing him, although it did so all the same. He did not expect to enrich his empty purse by mining twilight for its gold, rubies, and emeralds. The state of his purse held no interest for him. If he had any transaction with the setting sun, it was to mint a new metaphor for his journal. I resented him for his indifference to things I had only now, in my manhood, begun to think were within reach of my still-tentative grasp.

"The sky is fine tonight," he said, granting me that much of his regard.

I nodded and, taking my pipe and tobacco pouch from my pocket, offered him some Cavendish, which he declined—not with contempt for a luxury, but like a man with an appetite for something else.

"We are neighbors," he said, looking off in the direction of my hut.

"Nearly so."

"Almost too near, I would have thought."

"I'm sorry, Mr. Thoreau. I hadn't considered . . ."

"No matter," he replied, cracking his knuckles to signal a change of subject. "You have a fine window sash."

"Thank you."

"I used to admire it when it hung on Jim Healey's shack while he and the other Irish were building the Fitchburg line. They've moved on since." He snuffled like a man whose nose has just been visited by a gnat. "How much did you pay for it?"

I was unaware of the cost of the window sash or of anything else that had gone into the building of my shack.

"How much did Emerson pay, then?"

I could not tell if he had meant to mock me. He might have been merely curious. He took a keen interest in economy—nature's and mankind's both.

"They built a railroad so that the ladies hereabouts can go to Boston to buy a hat, when we have a perfectly good milliner in Concord," he jibed.

I recalled that Mistress Jeroboam had bought her hats in Richmond, where the latest folderol from Paris could be gotten. I must have said as much to Henry, because he began to fume.

"Why must we always look abroad for the cut of our clothes!" he sneered. "We can sew a button on as neatly as the French."

I thought then that he was needlessly opinionated where small matters were concerned.

"Can you weed a bean row with that one hand of yours?" he asked, looking at my shirt's empty cuff.

"I can."

"If you're not above bartering, we can do each other some good."

I REMEMBER THE FIRST TIME I went to Emerson's house to report on Henry's progress at Walden. I make us sound like a pair of conspirators, with myself as spy, but that was not the case. The older man was concerned for his protégé's welfare. They had been friends and correspondents since 1837. It was Emerson who had encouraged Henry to keep a journal, which he did until his death. Otherwise, the original thoughts of this original man would have mingled forever in the waters of Lethe, the universal forgetfulness. We have Emerson to thank for the many excellent works of natural history and ethics, especially *Walden; or, Life in the Woods*—a book that, if I may be permitted to indulge in clairvoyance—will be read after Walden Pond has been emptied and the woods thereabouts cut down.

Emerson's house was roomy and foursquare, like his philosophy. Two-storied, mansard-roofed, and white-clapboarded, "Bush," as he and his wife, Lidian, called it, was an easy walk across Mill-dam from Walden Pond.

The parlor could sometimes be noisy with opinions concerning nature's sovereignty, voiced by Henry, Emerson, and his Transcendental Club, which had made Bush its academy and Concord its omphalos, as Bronson Alcott, a "tedious archangel," liked to say.

I would listen to them debate the necessity of conformity, government, institutions, and religions. Once to my dismay, the club—to which Henry did not belong—argued the nature of reality. Emerson averred, "Mind is the only reality, of which men and all other natures are better or worse reflectors. Nature, literature, history, are only subjective phenomena." He might have been right, but I would argue—adducing the scars on Frederick Douglass's back and on my own—that the body, too, is a reality—importunate and undeniable. I was a simple man, only recently having escaped the nightmare from which there is seldom an awaking. My people live foremost in a physical world, where the Arcadia of thought and speculation is as far away as Eden from a cotton field. We must grub like Job.

I am straying from my purpose, which is to praise Henry David Thoreau. But perhaps I have not strayed far. Even now, he and I are bound to each other. I, more so than he, for he was the greater man—I readily admit it. I gave him something, however, that he would have lacked otherwise: knowledge—no matter how imperfect—of another order of humanity, another kind of man.

"What do you think of him?" Emerson asked on that September morning when I arrived at Bush and was shown by Mrs. Emerson into his study. I was frightened even then of speaking—ill or well—of one white person to another. A man will wear his chains long after they have been removed, in the same way one feels pain in a leg that has been cut off. "Go on, Samuel," Emerson said kindly. "What is your frank opinion of our friend Henry?"

I looked around the study and took courage in its simple furnishings, the profusion of books, the light falling without harshness onto the varnished floorboards, the desk where he had left an unfinished manuscript, one sentence of which I noted with especial approval: "I have only to endure."

"He walks——"

"Oh, Henry has always walked!" said Emerson, smiling broadly.

"He walks as if he means to leave something behind, but he always returns to the place whence he started. He walks as if he were fleeing the cruelest of drivers."

"I suppose he is," said Emerson thoughtfully. "It will wear out your boot soles if you try to keep pace with him."

"He talks while he goes."

"He's worth listening to, Samuel. And his health?"

"Well enough, I should say."

"He has consumption. But he will not rest himself. He is eating himself alive. Ellery Channing exhorted him to 'go out upon that'—Walden Pond, he meant—'build yourself a hut, & there begin the grand process of devouring yourself alive. I see no alternative, no other hope for you.' Neither do I, poor fellow. Henry is a meteor and will not last."

"He doesn't complain."

"No, there's no point. Nature's character is stoical, and Henry is a natural man. What does he say of the pond?"

"That it is deep."

Emerson laughed again. I could not see the joke, if joke there was. But in time, I would come to know the pond's dark depths and appreciate them.

"He lived here, at Bush, before going to the woods to live. He did odd jobs in return for his keep. Henry is a handyman; he knows how to use tools. He and his father built a house for the pencil works from wood huts left over by the Irish laborers on the Fitchburg Railroad. Well, you know he built that hut of his himself—or so he would have us believe. He had the assistance of George Curtis and Edmund Hosmer in raising it."

"I would not call it a hut," I said. I had lived in huts and had done without so much as a blanket. I had slept in an empty sack.

"His 'hut' is a symbol of his emancipation and, because of it, it needn't be barren to make his point," Emerson replied.

That was the difference between us. Henry's life, like his house, his sojourn in Walden Woods, and his night of imprisonment, were literature. I mean no disrespect to him or to those among my readers who love him. Henry was a fine man, maybe even a great one. I cherish his books as I do his memory. I admire the breadth of his thought, his indifference to the world's opinion, and his nonconformity. But he was free to do as he wished. We can never know how he would have stood the cow-skin lash, an overseer's fists, the galling chain, or the auctioneer's hammer, which seals the fate of negroes on the block—a block no less dire for us than it was for the English king who lost his head on one.

Those were the thoughts that tumbled pell-mell through

my brain. I did not speak them aloud—dared not, fearful that to be critical of his friend might prompt Emerson to renounce me. I lived in fear of the man hunters.

Lidian brought us tea, and, after having finished mine, I returned to the woods and my own hut. By Emerson's generosity, I enjoyed the luxuries of an iron stove, a planked floor, a washstand and bowl, a feather bed, and blankets to warm me through the cold Massachusetts winter I spent in Walden Woods—a warmth augmented by ardent spirits, the occasional gift of Nathaniel Hawthorne, when he came to visit us in Concord. Drinking nothing stronger than beer, Henry was happy to besot himself with sunsets or the view from Nawshawtuck Hill of shorn buckwheat fields red in the distance.

AUTUMNAL FIRES SWEPT THE HILLS, and soon the leaves would fall. Henry and I walked west from Walden Pond, across the Fitchburg tracks, and on to Bear Garden Hill, boots scuffling among the first leaves to have dropped. They lay in copper, gold, and russet heaps. We strayed among the fiddleheads, which would shed their fronds under the first snow, but now were green and moist. Henry admired them for possessing "the delicacy of a Fragonard," whose paintings he had seen in an album of copperplate reproductions belonging to Lidian Emerson.

"I would not mince about a rich man's salon," he said, "to ogle the king of France, much less an oil painting in a gilded frame. But a book is a democracy of sorts, and I am free to look at what I like."

Having never seen a Fragonard, I did not feel qualified to comment. My experience of painting was limited to the sturdy views of New England hanging in Emerson's study and some gaudy portraits of Jeroboam's ancestors, which, for all I know, he might have purchased—gold frames and all—for the sake of a doubtful pedigree. He had an acquisitive nature, and there was little he could not afford to buy.

"What do you say, Mr. Long? Is the view not worth the climb?"

"Call me Samuel."

"Good, and you must call me Henry."

I looked at the scenery, while Henry refined the ore of his keener perceptions into an aphorism for his journal.

"Nature has a taste for dainties as a woman does bonbons," he said, picking a sponge mushroom from the grass.

"I have never eaten a bonbon," I said pensively.

"They are not worth your regret, Samuel."

Who is Henry to decide what I should or should not regret? I thought. It was childish of me. I cared nothing for bonbons, but suddenly I worried over them like a dog a bone, which has no more nourishment than a stick.

"Our local barley sugar candies are treat enough."

With that assertion, he had settled the matter. We walked awhile in silence, except for what sounds the woods will make. He kicked a stone out of his path, and we listened to it tumble down the hillside.

So it was, during our first months together. Despite my promise to Emerson that I would befriend Henry during his time in the woods, I had taken a dislike to him. *Dislike* may be too strong a word for the disapproval I felt. I knew from Waldo and his acolytes how very good a man Henry was, for all his roughshod ways. He envied no one his station. He was as carefree as a bird and as abstinent as a Hindu. But still he nettled me.

What were his privations next to those that I had had to bear? His father owned a factory. Henry had gone to Harvard. Emerson was his patron. He would have wanted for little if he had been desirous of material comfort. I considered his abnegation willfulness, an ostentatious virtue as annoying as chastity. Henry lived poorly by the world's judgment, when he could have lived well. His renunciation was no better than that of a man who, having filled his stomach, throws away what is left of his meal in sight of a starveling. And I was the starveling!

Carping has no place in an elegy, but Henry could be insensitive. Did he not write in *Walden*: "It is hard to have a southern overseer; it is worse to have a northern one; but worst of all when you are the slave-driver of yourself"? He read that passage to me, as he did much of what he was writing in his journals at the time. Listening, I felt the heat of resentment mount like mercury in a thermometer, and I did what I could not have dreamed of doing when I was a bondman in Virginia: I contradicted a white man.

"It is much, much worse, Henry, to be driven by a vicious brute whom law and custom have given charge over one's life than by an inner demon," I said. I might not have used those words exactly; my education had only begun.

I could see that I had offended—no, *hurt* him, his feelings. Strange even now to write of feelings. It is said that negroes have none, any more than dogs do. On the contrary, I can assure you that we hate. Remarkably, we also manage to love when we can, although our hearts have been torn to pieces. We also feel pain, which is stronger than love—stronger than our hatred. Pain makes us afraid. One never gets used to it. The flesh can knot and welt and perhaps, in time, heal, but the mind remains raw—the voice within one's head a shriek. Henry's idea of a slave driver was on the line of a carnival barker or patent-medicine man, whose voice whipped up enthusiasm but drew no blood. For blood, one required a whip, a fist, a fence post, or an ax.

To his credit, Henry had understood me.

"You're right," he said, rising from the step in front of his little house to walk about his yard. He was a man who liked to combine his thinking with his walking. "Words seem to want to go their own way. It's their willfulness that's the trouble. Once you've begun to rock, even a hobbyhorse can run away with you!" he said, having returned to the step on which I sat. "I'm guilty, Samuel, of having made a metaphor of slavery with which to furnish my thought."

He was off again on his circumnavigation of the leaf-strewn yard—his ambit as narrow as a chicken run. But his mind was wide as the firmament. "Slavery is an idea; its overthrow must come from a countering idea."

By the time he returned to the doorstep, he had changed his mind again.

"No, we cannot end slavery with an idea, not even a glorious one. Those in the North who cheer Frederick Douglass and purchase his narrative will not shorten the term of human bondage by so much as a minute. I am not for war, nor am I for the indefinite postponement of justice in order to keep the peace."

Like Emerson, Henry was not afraid of contradicting himself. Perhaps his supple mind was capable of braiding diverse strands of thought into a rope with which to save a man or hang him.

Having again circled the yard, he stopped in front of me and, quoting from Douglass's autobiography, said: "'You have seen how a man was made a slave; you shall see how a slave was made a man.' Douglass became a man not by his wits—attempting to reason with Covey, the 'nigger-breaker,' who had just beaten him without mercy and was preparing to do so again—but with his fists. He fought the overseer and so disenthralled himself. His escape into the North was almost beside the point, for he was already free."

I said nothing, my mind a jumble.

"Sometimes the heart must become a fist, which it resembles." He smote his palm with his. "I'm afraid there is nothing I can teach you, Samuel!"

I could not guess his meaning. Did he judge me as intractable and hopelessly backward, or was the judgment delivered against himself—an acknowledgment of his shortcomings where other people were concerned? Or did Henry lament—his voice had been sorrowful—the inability of anyone to instruct another in what was most important and, conversely, the impossibility of ever knowing another's heart or mind?

But then he surprised me by making what seemed an apology for his having presumed to teach me about suffering and what the South calls its "peculiar institution."

"Being no more than a man, with many of the faults of that accursed species, I am bound to make mistakes. I shall depend on you, Samuel, to reprove the fault in me."

I nodded warily, while he took from his pocket a bone-handled jackknife.

"I can—on second thought—teach you to play mumblety-peg."

A NORTHERN WINTER IS ANOTHER KIND of bitterness. It has about it the Yankee character—rawboned, hard-bitten, and dour. One who is unused to it can feel as though he has been invaded by the earth itself—its flint and rocky soil, into which the recent dead cannot be laid till thaw. Henry was untroubled by the cold. Having spent most of his twenty-nine winters in Concord, he had become inured to it by his endless tramps. He knew the country-side in flower as well as under snow.

I recall the first time I saw him skating on the frozen river, together with Emerson and Hawthorne. He cut a figure like a scarecrow prone to pratfalls. Emerson was competent, Hawthorne skillful. Until recently, he and his wife, Sophia, had lived in Concord, at the Old Manse, but the rent had increased beyond their means. Residing now in Salem, Hawthorne would return to visit his literary friends.

The sky that afternoon was strangely colored. "Like pewter," Emerson described it; "like the heart after its first transgression," said Hawthorne; "like a fluke's when it has been left to rot," said Henry. They were literary men, and I could not fault them for their whimsicality. Had they been otherwise, they would have left no mark. Who would have heard of the economy of the mouse or the iniquity of the poll tax collected to subjugate the Mexicans if Henry's words had fallen short of his wisdom, had failed to stir the hearts of men and women in a measure equal to his own passion?

When they came off the river, their cheeks burnished and their beards grizzled with beads of ice, they stood awhile, flapping their arms like pump handles to get the blood flowing again and talking of this and that. They did not always speak like Transcendentalists or littérateurs. Sometimes they spoke as ordinary men do about commonplace things. It is an obvious remark for me to make, but most of us expect the great men among us to inhabit an elevated plane, from which they never depart. Henry could talk to Hawthorne about the pickerel in Long Cove, where Walden Pond bumps up against the Fitchburg tracks, as well as about Poe's latest tale. He could talk about crop yields and weather as easily as Paley's *Natural Theology*. Once to my surprise, I overheard him quarreling with Emerson over baseball and Cartwright's Knickerbocker Rules, after discussing the merits of Lyell's *Principles of Geology*.

Henry snuffled at ice crystals in his nose and said, "Last winter, I broke some ice on Swamp Bridge Brook and saw a shining city of steeples rising from the bottom of a floe." He wound his muffler tightly around his neck. "I've seen crystals in frost that resemble budding branches. There is a continuity throughout nature that is best expressed metaphorically."

"A leaf, a drop, a crystal, a moment of time, is related

to the whole, and partakes of the perfection of the whole. Each particle is a microcosm, and faithfully renders the likeness of the world," said Emerson, his voice trailing off toward infinity, where his thoughts tended.

"I sometimes wonder if we don't do reality a disservice with our metaphors," said Hawthorne, stamping his feet to warm them.

Many times I found their conversation tedious; they could make the game of baseball sound as serious as a parliamentary debate, and the local husbandry a gloss on Virgil's *Georgics*.

I was not an illiterate, thanks to Mistress S— and to my own painful and secret efforts to learn to read, but many years would pass before I could comprehend the books that lay scattered around me like pearls before swine or—less demeaning—crumbs before sparrows, whom Jesus loves. In 1846, I could read a seed catalogue, a book by Cooper or Defoe, the Bible and *The Pilgrim's Progress*, and poems by Whittier or Longfellow. I did not know what to make of Emerson's essays, which had not been shaped by a mind born in bondage, nor were easy to comprehend for one still fettered by custom and habit. I could no more think in new ways and to new purposes than I could build my house in the woods to appear otherwise than the hovels I had known in slavery.

A pious woman had given me a copy of Jonathan Edwards' "Sinners in the Hands of an Angry God." I had taken it from my pocket to read while Henry was writing in his journal. It was cold in his little house, and the iron stove was murmuring.

"What is that you're reading, Samuel?" he asked.

I told him and—to my surprise—he rose from his writing desk, tore the pamphlet from my hands, and threw it in the stove.

"That was my property!" I shouted. Strange to hear myself claim ownership when, until recently, I myself had been another's property.

He looked at me shamefaced and, shuffling in embarrassment, apologized. "Forgive me, Samuel. But it pained me to see you reading a tract that would scare you with a hell as real and fiery as *that*." He opened the stove door, and we watched in fascination while the fire waggled its tongues. "God is not angry!" he cried, his stoical upper lip showing teeth. He had sufficient Unitarianism in him to scorn fundamentalist Christian melodrama. "Hell is inside us: It is the pain we cause ourselves."

If I had not known in my shredded heart that hell was outside us, I would have agreed. Many years would pass before it would be mended. Like an article of clothing, however, the stitches—that ragged scar—would always be visible in my character.

I was wrong when I faulted Henry for having chosen to live in poverty—he would not have called it that—when he could have lived comfortably in his family's boarding-house in the village. I mistook him for a poseur, a dilettante of the ascetic life. At the time, I could not have said what he was. When I could distinguish gold from base metal, so to speak, I understood that his two years in the woods were—as he himself called them—an "experiment," which, having been concluded to his satisfaction, he did not need to belabor. His genius lay in his ability to live fully by living variously.

EARLY IN FEBRUARY, A CREW of one hundred men, mostly Irish, from the Tudor Ice Company, of Boston, arrived at Walden to harvest ice. I watched as they walked behind horse-drawn cutters, a pair of sharpened blades scoring pond ice instead of breaking sod. And then with saws, picks, gaffs, and tongs, other men cut blocks and loaded them onto sleds for the poor horses to haul to the icehouse. I pitied them their labor, watching their breath transpire into the cold air, as if they were giving up the ghost of themselves. Each day the men began merrily enough, but by evening, when the winter light was going, their jests turned to oaths. When the shadows had lengthened into darkness, their curses faded into a silence broken by the grunts of men and animals and the scoring of the ice.

Watching the horses slumped in harness beneath the driver's lash, I asked Henry, "Would you kill a man?"

"In a manner of speaking, or in actuality?"

"I'm asking if you could kill a man, if you had a reason to."

He resented the question. Perhaps it brought to earth an ethical choice he could never put into practice or a wish he could not gratify.

"What reason could there be?" he asked.

This man who had always looked me in the eye turned his to the vegetable and mineral world that lay open to his curiosity and would never pose a question that might shame him. I realized that the source of his strength and also of his weakness was nature—one that did not include the mass of ordinary men and women, regardless of how he might stand and pass the time of day with them. He studied nature, admired it, venerated and adored it. For him, there could be no higher order or realm.

"If you should be set upon by thieves . . ." I said to prod him into speech.

"I have nothing to steal," he said—smugly, I thought.

"By assassins, then." I persisted, wanting blood from the stone that his awkward self-consciousness had made of him at that moment.

"I could not ransom my life with theirs," he said after the smallest of hesitations.

"And to save me?" It was all I could do not to shout at this upright man, whose greatest wish, I believed at the time, was never to be thrust into a position where he could be forced to violate his principles.

I left him to them and walked to the sandy edge of the pond to watch men untroubled by philosophy or religion beyond a rough-and-ready acceptance of the faith of their Irish mothers or thoughts beyond a warming draft by the fire at Hartwell Bigelow's tavern, near the burial ground, where teamsters and the local rowdies drank steadily toward forgetfulness.

The hour was at hand when the men could put away their tools and tramp into Concord, where they were lodged. They walked in silence, the sweat inside their clothes turning to ice. Curious, I followed them into town, while night sealed the woods with a darkness thick as pitch. Most of the icemen headed for the light that fell through the tavern window onto the iron-colored snow. Bigelow's creaking door announced their arrival into the noisy room, whose walls seemed to tremble in the lamp- and firelight.

I thought of Henry, alone in his cabin, and hated myself for having tried to shame him. He meant me well and wished for all the satisfaction of a life well spent. If I saw a chasm yawn between us, the fault might have been my own. I did not understand how a mind could waver between alter- natives—a strange notion for a slave, who must be constant in his submission to authority. A bondman has no more use for a subtle mind or a personality than a hitching post.

The icemen pushed in among workmen from Concord's pipe and bucket factories, the tinsmith's and blacksmith's, the coopery and tannery. I could disentangle from the general din the accent peculiar to New England, together with a sardonic Irish and an imperious German. The men were a boisterous, irreligious lot, whose noise increased with each whiskey glass or pint, the cacophony min- gling—if sounds and odors can be said to mingle—with the smell of peat, tobacco, and a ferment of roots, hops, and spruce, released from a fiery rum concoction by the red-hot mulling pokers. My eyes watered in the smoke- filled room, and soon my head felt light, although I had only a glass of porter planted between my elbows where they rested on the rough-hewn bar.

On either side of me sat an Irishman from County Clare. They were reminiscing fondly about the river Shan- non—finer than the Concord or the Charles; the Cliffs of

Moher—grander than the Palisades, though neither man had seen the Hudson River; Galway Bay—lovelier than Dorchester Bay, which they had glimpsed from the heights of south Boston; and the geniality of an Irish hearth that burned peat from an Irish bog. They spoke to each other between gulps of raw whiskey, which lacked the taste, color, and fire of the venerable Jameson, as though I were not a man sitting between them, but a pane of window glass.

I was accustomed to living as if I took up no more space or air than a dog does—less, for a dog in a southern household may be privileged. Let us say, then, that my conspicuousness had been on the order of a hoe or, since I had been a kitchen slave, a saucepan—necessary, but not really seen and rarely appreciated. I grew to resent the micks sitting on either side of me. Like anyone else, I could be contemptuous of others, although I knew enough to keep my scornful thoughts unspoken.

There are noble hearts among us. There are also hearts as pitiless as sleet. To maintain that all negroes are innocent is as pernicious as to declare us all guilty of iniquity. The former attitude consigns us to a state of perpetual childhood, the latter to savagery; both justify the strict governance and chastisement of our overseers. It is the commonly held opinion that we will be incapable of harming ourselves or others just as long as our chains are not struck off.

I glared at the man seated on my right, who, with a careless shrug of his broad shoulders, had caused the porter to spill from my glass.

I am not a big man, but, when a young one, I could have held my own against most other men in a fair fight or a dirty one if I could have disenthralled myself of the habit of abjection and found the will to unfetter my strength, which was constrained by fear.

"What's the matter, nigger?" he asked, his eyes glinting the way eyes will in spite.

"I am not a nigger," I said in a voice whose quaver I barely managed to control.

"You sure do look like one. Does this boy look like a darkie to you, Colin?"

"He does and all."

"Then what in the hell are you looking at?" demanded the irascible Irishman, whose name was Tyrrell, after having set his glass down on the bar with a bang.

I wanted to kill the thick-skulled galoot, and remembered the prickly exchange of views I had had with Henry earlier that night. I wished he were there so that he might wrestle with his principles. Notwithstanding his narrow build and awkwardness, Henry was hardened by manual labor and his habitual tramps and climbs in the mountains north of the village. Knots of muscle stood out on his calves like hawsers. He could have been a teamster or a porter if he had not been an idler—a description he cherished as the mark of a man bent on self-discovery. Henry did not sponge or beg for money or favors. If the world considered him shiftless, he could say, with some truth, that he hurt no one nor lived at another's expense. (His self-reliance was partly self-delusion, as it must be for any mortal.) Naturally, Henry would not have bothered to defend himself against the village backbiters, who lived within the sound of Emerson's voice but were nevertheless deaf to it.

Henry's presence in the tavern would have made no difference: Roughnecks came and went at the urging of sobriety and intoxication. Indifferent to the niceties of polite combat, they would have murdered the pair of us. And yet, fretted as I was by an accrual of humiliation, I wanted to strike them and, perversely, I wanted *to be struck by them*. I felt a kind of self-hatred, for which I cannot even now account.

I must have tensed; maybe I went as far as to raise myself to my full height where I stood between the two Irishmen at the bar. The one called Colin must have sensed what I meant to do. He took me by the wrist. I thought he meant to throw me or to twist my arm behind my back and break it. Then I saw something in his eyes I could not interpret: not fear or excitement, sadness or understanding, but something partaking of them all. I don't know what I saw in his blue eyes. I let my body relax and my shoulders slump—not in submission, but as a man will who lets out a deep sigh after a storm of emotion has been spent.

Tyrrell went to the cask to draw himself a mug of lager.

Colin winked at me—he may have smiled—and made a joke of my black skin. "Will it rub off?"

He did not mean to insult me, and I was not insulted. He looked at the palm of his hand, the one that had held my wrist, as if he expected to see his skin turned the color of my own.

"I never touched a black man before," he said shyly.

I was thrilled to hear him call me a man. He was loutish; there was nothing in the least refined about his manners or his words. I could not imagine his life, but I guessed it was hard, maybe even mean. I had heard that the Irish were considered little better than my own people and that indentured servitude, while of only seven years' duration—time unmarked by neither whip nor auction—wore down body and soul. I looked into his eyes—he did not seem to mind as his friend Tyrrell had minded—and tried to read his thoughts.

None can know another's mind. Nonetheless, we do speak and write of others as if we have known them well. What can Melville have known of Ahab, or Edgar Poe of Usher, or Hawthorne of Dimmesdale? And yet they have written of them in the belief that we possess a common soul. So it is that I have found within me courage to speak of and for various persons met during my stay in Walden Woods as though I had sounded to the bottom of them . . . as if I had sifted them fine.

Colin studied my face like an unlettered child straining to make sense of chalk marks on a slate. Then he shook his head and said, "It must be a strange thing to have been born a negro."

"Yes," I replied, not knowing what I meant by it.

Tyrrell returned with his beer and took his place at the bar.

"You and the coon palavering, are you?" he asked his friend brusquely.

"Let him be for Christ's sake!" growled Colin. "He's not a bad fellow"—he finished the sentence with a wink at me—"for a blackie."

Tyrrell wiped the foam from his mustache and, with a splinter, picked at his teeth.

I wish that I could write that I walked back to Colin's rooming house and, away from the commotion of Bigelow's tavern, we talked like two people determined to know each other better. I might have tried to speak of my feelings and thoughts when I had belonged to another man—you cannot imagine the shame of such a confession. In turn, he could have told me about the poverty and hunger of the Irish, whom even the potatoes had failed. But we would have no such conversation.

If I seem preoccupied by my own story, I believe that it is as necessary to Henry's own as weft and weave are to a basket. I am not mentioned in his account of his sojourn in Walden Woods. I was not important to his experiment. I might have spoiled the design of his story. Who knows what thoughts pass through the mind of an author? Henry will be remembered, while what I write here will be forgotten soon enough. In any case, I am certain not to write it half so well. Henry had a genius for making common things seem monumental. In his work, an acorn assumes the proportions of the Taj Mahal. My pen, I fear, would turn the Taj Mahal into an acorn.

By March, the ice taken by Frederic Tudor's men had returned to Walden Pond's Deep Cove. Hands in our pockets, Henry and I were walking along the margin of stiff marsh grass when his attention, concentrated on a snow-white ermine worrying a shrew, was caught by something red twenty or thirty yards from shore.

"What is it?" I asked.

His eyes were sharper than mine; his habit of looking closely had doubtless made them so. His range of vision was remarkable: He could detect a lofted eagle whose compact shadow slipped across a distant hillside as readily as a garter snake sliding through the grass at his feet.

"It looks like a piece of red flannel," he said.

He had already started toward it, cautiously as anyone uncertain of his footing and the thickness of the ice would. It was too early in the year for it to make a noise like gun-shot—that sharp crack or boom one hears in late March or early April, when the thaw begins. But still, the ice splin-tered some when it took a man's weight.

"Go carefully!" I shouted as he neared the red rag. "The ice is new."

I watched as he got down on his hands and knees and scraped with the blade of his hand. He took off his hat, brought his face near the frosted pane of ice, and peered at what lay underneath it: a drowned boy—child of one of the woodcutters living by the Assabet River, which flows into the Concord. It was the end of his scarf Henry had seen, raised stiffly above the surface like a frozen pennant. The clarity of Walden Pond's ice, which Frederic Tudor coveted, had made a kind of window, through which Henry saw the boy's face and—in my fancy—the boy saw his.

"Go get Sam Staples," shouted Henry.

I hurried into town and brought the sheriff back with me—the morbid and the curious trailing noisily behind us like the rattle of a snake.

Later, at Anderson's Market, where Henry and I had gone to buy flour, lard, potatoes, and candles, village men were vociferously airing opinions on how the Carlson boy, missing since fall, had come to be in the pond. Some believed a renegade had murdered him and put the body into the water before it froze. Others suspected the Irish ice cutters because of their allegiance to the Roman church, which wished all good Protestants harm. Henry snorted at this latest proof of the lunacy and prejudice of vox populi.

"They tell a story hereabouts of an iron chest lying at the bottom of the pond that can be seen, on occasion, floating toward shore before it sinks out of sight again," said Henry while we were crossing the Mill-dam on the way back to our woods. "Water has reasons of its own; the things of the natural world carry on as if humans had not yet been thought of—as if God had ceased in His creation before Adam, who, according to Scriptures, was made after the fashion of a brick."

Henry's misanthropy was never more pronounced than just after the drowning, as though a seam had opened inside him, wide enough for a vein of ice to clot. It may have been there since the death of his brother and required only this latest proof of God's indifference and men's spite to chill his genial spirit.

One night at the end of winter, while I was inside my hut, reading by candlelight from Abraham Rees's *The Cyclopædia; or, Universal Dictionary of Arts, Sciences, and Literature,* lent to me by Emerson, the boy's father shouldered open my door with a crack of splintering wood. He was well beyond sobriety, appeals to reason, or caring whether or not there was one negro less in Concord. Experience had taught me that safety lay in silence. Carlson had an ax, with which in peaceable days he used to cut down trees. It would serve, as well, to cut down a man.

"Did you kill my boy?" he snarled, spittle dripping onto his unshaved chin.

I shook my head sadly. "No, sir, I did not."

I pitied him his loss and, in spite of myself, admired his violent love. If my own death could have resurrected the boy and turned his gray face to the rosy tints of childhood, I would have laid my head upon the table and bid the father chop.

The lamplight shone upon the blade of his ax. Carlson rocked on his heels like someone under the strain of a great uncertainty: Would he give way to despair or to desperation, emotions that led to quite different ends? The hut seemed choked—or rather, I did, as though the flue had been closed and the smoke from the stove had begun to spill out into the narrow room. Carlson appeared bewildered as Abraham was after God had demanded the slaughter of his son. He dropped the ax; I heard the dull sound of its striking the floor. I beheld it as if it were the sacrificial knife, or a relic of holiness. It was only an ax, dulled by the flesh of trees. Carlson slumped in my chair—he was welcome to it. I moved to get Hawthorne's whiskey, but repented. The man had had enough—more than enough would not have consoled him. Nothing could console him. I could read that much in his stricken face. I hesitated, wanting to put my hand on his arm, but I was afraid and put it in my pocket instead so as not to be tempted to comfort him again.

After a while, he stood, picked up his ax, and left without a word or even so much as a glance at me. He had already returned—in Emerson's phrase—to his "private music," which would be ever after sad. I set the door roughly in the broken jamb. Too shaken to rest, I sat up during much of the night and read from the Book of Psalms. I remember this verse from the forty-ninth: "My mouth shall speak of wisdom; and the meditation of my heart shall be of understanding. / I will incline my ear to a parable: I will open my dark saying upon the harp."

Only the month before, Henry had played the "ice harp" with stones thrown, one by one, onto the frozen pond. Air, trapped inside its icy chambers, resounded in an eerie music. That night in my hut, I imagined a dirge played in the place where the Carlson boy had drowned— a lugubrious melody of stones falling on frozen water.

The next afternoon when I returned from Emerson's house with a book by Audubon for Henry, I found my cabin door had been mended.

Thereafter, I would always think that a tincture of death had stained Walden Pond as tea leaves do water when they are brewed.

"Death is in the pond," I would say to Henry, as if I still believed the stories I had heard as a child from Haitian slaves of the supernatural world, in which the Loa dwelled.

"Nonsense!" he would reply, his voice raised in impatience.

Even now I think about that boy staring walleyed through the frosted window at the sky under which he used to play, tramp hills and meadows, climb the ancient trees, walk to school, to church, to town, to Walden Pond, at every season of the year, for the handful of years that had been his. I picture him caught in a net of rank bottom weed—chained up in it—while the pond freezes over. Later on, a disturbance beyond even Henry's power of audition unshackles him and sets him wandering, dreamily, through Walden's icy veins. Even now, long after he was raised from the water through a hole in the ice chopped by his father, I sometimes imagine him on his way, passing through underground sluices into the Assabet, the Concord, and the ocean, where he is swimming still among a silent host of drowned mariners. And I could never see the fields painted red with sorrel in June without remembering with a shudder the frozen bit of scarf.

II

ESPITE THE SMALL SOCIETY of Concord to which I was admitted, I felt lonely. I knew no one well. My acquaintances, thus far, had been of the white race. The difference between us could not be forgotten, however much it might be ignored. I wanted to talk to another black man. To have done so as a free man, albeit a fugitive, would have been as if to speak to another of my people for the first time, without inhibition or fear of the lash. We would be free to like each other or not, according to our different characters and temperaments. We would have been two persons instead of a pair of barely distinguishable beings on the order of beasts, maltreated and despised. Finally, I asked Henry if he knew of another negro living in the vicinity.

"There's old Jake, who mucks out the livery stable, but I doubt you would have anything in common beside your race. Arnold Knowles, elder son of a carter, lives out on the Cambridge Turnpike. And Joseph—I don't recall his surname, if I ever knew it. He's a dogsbody at the printer and engraver's and stays with his sister and her brood out by

Little Goose Pond. We tilled Hawthorne's garden before he and Sophia moved into the Old Manse." He paused and then said, "There are a number of negro housemaids hereabouts. . . ."

He glanced curiously at me. He would not have known how to leer, and would never have pulled so indecent a face, if he had. Henry's manners were rough because he considered them superfluous to living, but his mind and heart were sound.

I had seen Jake bent over a horse's hoof to rid it of a stone. I had seen the carter and his son driving down Main Street, the wagon sagging on its leaf springs under a load of barrels. I had never thought to speak to them. But Joseph, who apprenticed at the printing shop, might be congenial. He had been manumitted when his owner, thrown from a horse that had been struck by lightning, freed his slaves, lest God Almighty's aim improve. So we became acquainted.

"You are Mr. Emerson's hired man," said Joseph during our first encounter.

"I can expect nothing better," I grumbled.

I was indulging in self-pity like a man in a tub of hot water after weeks of roughing it. I have been guilty of feeling put-upon and aggrieved. I would like to blame my disgruntlement on hardships suffered in my youth, but I suspect it has more to do with weakness.

"Better a hired man than an enslaved 'boy,'" Joseph replied tartly.

I did not care for his remark, which I considered rude to one who had taken him into his home and confidence. I could be patronizing, only I could not see it. In those days,

I was often blinded by resentment that would flare up like phosphorus on a matchstick.

Joseph chided, "You make yourself small, Samuel, if you can't admire good people who also happen to be white."

He was right, and I would have blushed for shame had the color of my skin allowed it. But his reproof had irked me, no matter that it was well-meant and deserved. I stood and turned my back on him. I remained thus until I heard his chair scrape against the rough floorboards, his heavy tread making for the door, and the door open and softly close. He left without another word. I hated him for having risen above shouting and the melodramatic slamming of the door. He had not goddamned me, although I had deserved it and, in his place, would have goddamned him.

Emerson would have done better by Henry to have hired the "dogsbody" to look after him. Joseph understood, as I did not, the difference between service and servility. The former can be dignified; the latter must be hateful and abject. Perhaps I was too young to have made such a distinction: I was only twenty-two or -three; the date of my birth is a mystery, as it is for most of my people. I do know that I came into the world during one of the coldest of Virginia winters, when water froze in ditches and in washbowls.

I kept to myself, avoiding Henry and Emerson both. Sitting in my cabin, I could hear the pond ice begin to crack. While the days lengthened and the sun grew near, the ice would shrink, together with the continents of snow on fields and meadows from Pine Hill to Mount Misery. I could hear the crack of rifle fire, too, as hunters stalked rabbits, squirrels, deer, and canvasbacks arriving from the Chesapeake to nibble our pond weed. I also heard a thin music coming from Henry's cabin; he liked to play his flute while standing at the window overlooking the pond. Regardless of his assertion that he could teach me nothing, I knew that I had much to learn from him, but, at that time, I preferred ignorance to a disciple's veneration.

THE DAY CAME WHEN I WAS SICK of my own company and ashamed of my peevishness. I was, as Henry had said of me, "well on the way to misanthropy." What is your reproof, I thought, but the pot calling the kettle black? "Solitude should be a temporary retreat from society, but not a substitute for it," he went on to say. In any case, I had neglected him and was determined to pay him a visit in his cabin.

The lowering sun was turning the pond water to gold when I set out through the copse from Bare Peak, where I had my dwelling. Three days of rain had beaten the ground into mud. Enraged by my trespass, squirrels chittered and jays jeered. Something rustled furtively in the grass. Wading unseen among the pond's reeds and rushes, a bittern made a noise like a stone falling into a well.

"You have an ear for native songs," Henry had once said—as handsome a compliment as one was likely to hear from him.

I had replied, "Anyone who has worked in the fields and woods from before the sun has risen until after it has set, week in and week out, year after year, with only the shouts and curses of the driver to fill his ears, will end up listening intently to the sounds of unfettered nature."

I write those words now, but I could not possibly have said them then. In truth, I cannot recall what words I had at my command. It was long ago. I have read mightily since my year in Walden Woods. I have wrestled with Emerson and Thoreau. I have chewed on such dry morsels as Mr. Whately serves in his *Elements of Rhetoric*. I have read most everything by Edgar Poe, Herman Melville, and by my old friend Hawthorne, with more pleasure than I have taken in the essays of my two erstwhile mentors.

"Reading is our recompense for having only one life to live," said Emerson—or maybe it was Hawthorne who said it. Memory is treacherous like pond ice when it has begun to thaw.

I knocked at Henry's door; his cottage had only one. The house was quiet, except for what sounds a house will sometimes make when the atmosphere changes, the timbers clench, or the dirt underneath grows restless. I put my ear to the door and strained to hear a noise betray a human presence within. All was silent.

"Henry! Henry Thoreau!" I shouted, knocking harder. "Are you all right?"

I heard a muttering that I could make no sense of it, but I was sure the voice belonged to Henry. I opened the door and went inside. Unlike me, he did not keep his door locked. I kept mine so because of the novelty of having one to lock, with none in the small world of Concord to forbid it.

Henry lay abed under blankets, shaking with fever. Damp shocks of his brown hair lay pasted to the high forehead; his color was hectic; his lips were chapped and bitten, his bluish gray eyes unnaturally bright.

I leaned over him and called his name. He was elsewhere. Anchor weighed, he was adrift in the current that carries us into the country of the sick. From snatches of a tune he sang, he must have been on the Merrimack with his brother, John, in their homemade boat. They had traveled together, during the summer of 1839, fifty miles down the Concord River and onto the Merrimack.

Delirious in his sickbed, Henry sang, "Row, brothers, row, the stream runs fast, / The rapids are near and the daylight's past!" And he would talk to Ellen Sewall, who stayed at the Thoreau boardinghouse when she visited her grandmother, Mrs. Ward. Henry adored the dark and pretty girl from Scituate.

I filled a washbowl, mopped his feverish brow, and wet his lips. His sunken cheeks made his beak of a nose more prominent. He thrashed about, trying to lift his head from the damp pillow.

"Water," he said in a voice like sand.

I gave him some.

"Ice," he said. "I'm parched."

The ice had gone from Walden. The nearest icehouse was at Fresh Pond, on the road to Boston. I thought of the icemen and their cold harvest shipped by boat to the Carolinas, New Orleans, to Calcutta and Bombay to chill a rich man's sherbet.

"I'm dying of thirst," he said, licking his cracked lips.

The philosopher lay helpless against the body's overthrow, while the ice that had grown all winter outside his window was slaking the thirst of a plantation owner or a maharaja.

Suddenly, I recalled the ice at Long Cove, left by Tudor's men because of imperfections that would have made it unprofitable to haul to market. Packed with coarse meadow hay and roofed over with boards, the ice, or some remnant of it, might have survived into the spring. I hurried through the darkness to the cove, carrying with me Henry's mattock and a wooden pail. Wrenching off a board, I found enough ice to fill it. By moonlight, the inert block looked dull. In sunlight, it would have been green.

Is it not strange that water left standing will turn putrid but if frozen will stay fresh for a thousand years? Might it not mean that ice—water's coarser nature—is, in actuality, the liquid element's transfiguration, partaking of eternity? Henry's thoughts, not mine.

I carried the pail to the cottage and, with the ice, made compresses, which, in a short while, checked Henry's rising temperature. I changed his bedding and clothes and cleaned his thin body. I had cared for my former master's children, performing small intimacies that, if they had not been sick, would have gotten me hanged. On several occasions, I tended Jeroboam when he had been drunk. Next morning, he would be especially severe with me for having witnessed his humiliation. Ministering to Thoreau that evening, I felt again the shame of Noah's son Ham, who had seen his father drunk and naked and had been cursed for it.

I fell asleep in Henry's chair, with his journal open on my lap. I had been reading nothing more interesting than a page of bookkeeping concerning the cost of his having set himself up in the woods. I found the prosaic entries restful. One cannot always be bogged down by ethical and philosophical speculations. I would have welcomed a novel by Sir Walter Scott or Hawthorne's *Twice-Told Tales*.

In the morning, Henry was only a little improved. I gave him iced water to sip and left him to rest while I searched among the brambles for the blackberries he loved, but it was still too early in the season. At the pond, I encountered a boy carrying a fishing pole. I gave him a one-cent piece, which satisfied him, and sent him to Emerson's house.

"Tell Mr. Emerson that Mr. Henry is sick at his cabin. Tell him Samuel said he was to come, please, if he can."

Lidian arrived instead, bringing elderberry syrup and cold red sumac tea, a sovereign remedy for fever and chills. She had also brought a bottle of barley wine "to fortify him."

"Mr. Emerson has gone to Brook Farm to inspect the damage." The main house of the Transcendentalist utopia founded by George and Sophia Ripley and Hawthorne had caught fire the month before. "He won't return until tomorrow. I thought I should look in on Mr. Thoreau."

Lidian Emerson was a slight woman—some would have called her gaunt—and in poor health ever since the scarlet fever. It had left her head feeling "hot ever after." She would not indulge her maladies, but fought beside her husband for his causes. Henry was drawn to her like a needle to a lodestone. I greatly admired her simplicity and strength. What is more, she called me "Mr. Long" or, sometimes, "Mr. Samuel," with a regard that was affectionate and sincere. She was not one of those women of the Concord sorority who hid an atom of condescension behind an unfailing show of politeness toward negroes.

"He's been asleep this last hour," I told her while she pulled off her gloves.

She laid a competent hand on Henry's brow. She had nursed her own four children in sickness, and, one of them, Waldo, she had watched as he embarked on the sickness unto death. She was satisfied by the treatment I had been giving Henry.

"You've done all that can be done, Mr. Long," she said matter-of-factly. "The crisis is past, and I don't believe the doctor need be sent for. Will you stay until he is well again?"

I felt momentarily put-upon but relented when I realized that it was for such a mischance as Henry's illness that her husband had installed me in his woods.

I nodded in the affirmative.

"If he should take a turn for the worse, please send word to me at Bush, and I will bring the doctor."

She felt Henry's forehead once again, looked him over critically, and left him in my care, along with the barley wine, which I myself drank.

My gaze was drawn to Henry's flute. It was a lovely thing of auburn-colored fruitwood and ivory. In all that stark room, there was nothing else so magnetic. It seemed out of place, like a velvet cushion in a monk's cell. I knew nothing of music except the songs of tribulation and deliverance sung by the slaves and the quadrilles, cotillions, and polkas danced by our "betters." Heard outside in the yard through tall windows stained gold by the light from the candelabras, the music had tumbled brightly over our misery like a bride walking unsullied through an ash pit.

Henry gave me a gold watch in gratitude for having nursed him back to health. Later, he admitted that it was of no value to him; he claimed to be indifferent to time as it is measured by clocks. He regretted having made me a present of it, fearing that it would "throw a chain round my neck more galling than a slave's iron collar." But I was happy to have it and would not give it back to him. I dreamed of one day owning a gold fob and, perhaps, a diamond to decorate it.

When Henry was well again, we walked to Egg Rock, at the confluence of the Sudbury and Assabet rivers, where they enter the Concord. There seven years earlier, he and his brother, John, had embarked on their excursion. They had feasted on bream and passenger pigeon during two weeks on the Merrimack and Concord, a boyish adventure that would do nothing to change the world or their own uncertain future. But at that moment in their brief histories, they came as near to giddiness and the folly of love as they ever would. Their mutual hopes of winning Miss Sewall's hand had yet to be dashed. While they rowed or sailed the rivers in their gaily painted boat, time was held in suspension and gravity forbore to weigh too heavily on them. Afterward, Henry wrote a book about their boat trip to the White Mountains.

The White Mountains remain, although I have never seen them, as does Egg Rock. In their season, rushes and wild flags still grow in the shadow it casts on the grassy bank. Aspens and alders are still leaning over the leisurely, meandering Concord, which the Algonquians call

"Meadow River." The abutments of the North Bridge, where Lexington and Concord militias bloodied British redcoats, stand defiantly in the river. Bream continue to swim and passenger pigeons to mob the sky. But Miss Sewall bestowed her hand on another, and by the time I went to live in the woods near Henry, his brother had died of tetanus. Now Henry, whom we once thought as perdurable as Egg Rock, the abutments of the North Bridge, and the rivers that flow from the continent into the Atlantic—he, too, has vanished—an unscheduled departure into regions where the clock does not strike or the bell toll the hour. We can only hope that Henry, who chafed at time's regulation, is satisfied.

His hour not yet come, he was sitting with his back against the rock.

"The stone feels warm," he said luxuriously while I stared at the river with an intentness usually reserved for great mysteries.

Always I have been drawn to the water's edge. To stand where one element gives way to another restores my belief in possibility. It must be what Blanchard felt when he made the first balloon ascent—not as it rose into the sky above Paris, but just moments before, when it was still tethered to the Champ-de-Mars.

Henry might loaf, but his mind was never idle. One might have thought him sunk in the pleasure of that moment by the river, but his mind was picking it apart with the assiduity of a cotton gin.

"Does the sun feel obliged to warm the rock so that I may sit comfortably with my back against it, or is this pleasant warmth only an instance of accidental good-ness—an unwitting act of kindness shown to me? And if the sun is unconcerned by my well-being—if, in fact, it acts on the world without awareness or intention—am I any less indebted to it? The universe is probably unaware of my existence by the Concord River, in Massachusetts, on the third day of May, in the year 1846. What matters is that *I* am aware of it."

"The first time a fish knows anything of men is when it gets yanked up from the bottom at the end of a string," I said with homely wisdom while admiring the cardinal flowers.

"A rude awakening for the poor fish," he said. "To behold the face of its god for the first time and see there only pitilessness."

Henry joined me on the riverbank, where we amused ourselves by skipping stones. I admit that I tried to outskip his. I was eager to beat him, while Henry did not care whether or not he won. He was ambitious for his mind's sake, never for those things for which most men yearn. Brothers have fallen out over a woman, but I doubt Henry objected to John's infatuation for Ellen Sewall. Henry was a gentleman in all but his clothes and manners, which were not rude, but rustic, and never intended to provoke the villagers, who considered him a crank. It would not have occurred to him to count his "skips" or mine while our stones glanced off the surface of the water.

Not content for long to dwell on the surface of things, he felt the need to peer into the depths—of the cosmos as William Herschel beheld it anew, of reality as Plato had conceived of it, of the earth as James Hutton grasped it. Fingering the skipping stone he had been about to throw, he said, "Think of it! This pebble is millions of years old! And where we're standing was once the bottom of a great ocean. The earth is not changed catastrophically, but gradually, not by sudden conversion, but by reasonable motions toward a new condition. Who can say whether the place to which all tends is better or worse than whence they came?"

Henry mused on the stone, which he seemed to be weighing on the palm of his hand, while I went back to skipping them. I was happy to watch them bound five, six, seven times before sinking to the bottom, where they—to Henry's mind—longed to be at rest.

"Objects in nature," he said, "have a kind of nostalgia that seeks to return them to their former places in time. Life is an endless to-and-fro, a desire to stay and a wishing to be gone."

He continued his apostrophe to the stone until I shut my ears to his voice, which had become more insistent and annoying than the drone of a wasp. Most of us must keep talking, afraid that, in the silence that rounds our lives, death will come like a shivaree, derisive and clamoring. But I sometimes longed to hear the foolishness of ordinary people.

AT SHATTUCK'S STORE, WHERE WE WENT that afternoon to replenish our flour, lard, paraffin, and salt, we encountered Emerson, who carried a bolt of blue muslin under his arm.

"Our Edith is to have a new frock," he said, and, in the

next breath, he continued irrelevantly, "I fear we'll see rain before the day is out."

"Why should you fear it?" asked Henry to nettle him.

"It is something one says when he can think of nothing else," Emerson replied irritably. "I wouldn't care to spend my days worrying about my every word's effect on posterity."

This, from a man who spoke as though he had an amanuensis in his pocket!

"How did you find conditions at Brook Farm?" asked Henry, ignoring the rebuke.

"The fire bell rang its death knell. I'm sorry for it, although neither of us could quite believe in Brook Farm as Utopia."

"I'd rather keep bachelor's hall in hell than go to board in heaven," replied Henry.

Emerson beamed at his protégé.

"The farm was no better than a plantation," said Henry. "Hawthorne paid a thousand dollars to join the Ripleys and slaved for six months shoveling cow manure before he quit the place in disgust."

Emerson sniffed, saying, "I fear that the communal ideal will always be a kind of genteel slavery for people like us."

I resented his patrician air and wished his kind could wake up one morning on the clay floor of one of Jeroboam's shacks.

"If you have the time, I'd like you both to meet someone," said Emerson.

"I promised Hosmer I'd tar the bottom of his boat," Henry replied, excusing himself. "I'll see you tomorrow, Samuel."

Henry ambled toward the river, taking his parcels with him.

I followed Emerson to Freemasons' Hall, where I first met William Lloyd Garrison.

"YOU SHOULDN'T HAVE URGED Fourier's communal ideal on Hawthorne and the Ripleys," Emerson chided Garrison, the Boston abolitionist and publisher of *The Liberator*. "The graft could never have taken on an American stock."

"They were too ambitious and unnecessarily extravagant," replied Garrison with some heat. "The cost to build the Phalanstery bankrupted the community, or nearly so. Meat, fish, and butter had disappeared from the refectory tables before the behemoth burned down, while the joy of laboring for the common good had been replaced by communal drudgery."

"In any case, Brook Farm is finished and won't rise again from its ashes," said Emerson.

Leaving them to argue the merits of associationism, I wandered into the library, where I was startled to see Joseph, with a hammer in his hand. He was equally surprised to see me there.

"Mr. Long," he said with what I thought was a hint of ridicule. "What brings *you* to the Lyceum?"

I did not know how I should answer him. Had I said that I was there to see the books, he might have thought that I meant to show my superiority to one who was clearly there to mend a shelf. On the other hand, if I were to make an excuse—if I were to tell him I had stepped into the library by chance, he might have gotten the idea that I knew full well I had no business there. Self-consciousness had hobbled me. So I lied. How often have I done so to forestall a shame that I did not deserve but—with the uneasiness of a man who is watched—could almost believe that I did?

"I'm here with Mr. Emerson," I said at last. "I'm helping him carry his packages." The packages were mine, and I realized with a pang that I had cast myself once more in the role of a bondman. "Mr. Garrison told me you were in the library. I thought I'd say hallo."

He noticed the hammer in his hand and appeared not to know what to do with it. I laid my hand on a copy of John Stuart Mill's *A System of Logic*, and, in turn, Joseph laid his on Asa Mahan's *Scripture Doctrine of Christian Perfection*. The moment was awkward for both of us. I could not see how to extricate myself. The doorway leading to the main room might have been on the other side of a snake-infested swamp. We stood facing each other for what seemed an age while sounds that ordinarily escape notice grew loud: The clock ticked, its seconds falling like hailstones; the oak shelves groaned; and the books, their thin, papery voices, whispered like a congress of old men.

"Have you been well, Joseph?" I asked, finding the room impossibly crowded, though we were its sole occupants.

"I have been well," he said in the stately way of ancient negroes.

"And your sister and her brood?" I asked.

"They are also well. I hope you are enjoying your life in the woods."

Did he mean to ridicule me? I could not decide, but I thought it best to remain civil.

"Very much so," I replied.

"I'm glad to hear it."

With an ostentatious gesture, I fished the gold watch out of my pocket by its chain and said, "I must be going. Mr. Emerson will want his packages."

Joseph nodded slyly, as if at Emerson's porter. I turned and left the room. No sooner had I crossed its threshold than the sound of hammering resumed. I could not remember the cause of our estrangement. Perhaps neither did he.

"Mr. Long, Mr. Emerson has been telling me of your former life of bondage. I wonder if you'd allow me to bring that story to the attention of readers of *The Liberator*. Slave narratives are the gunpowder that will help us destroy that despicable institution."

I glared at Emerson. I had no desire to put my painful recollections at the service of abolition. I was sorry for the millions of my race in captivity, but I had closed that chapter of my life and had no wish to reopen it. I did not want to be another "well-spoken negro" of the sort that was made much of in the South, as though a monkey, by the perseverance of its owner, had been made to talk. There is nothing so wounding to the spirit as to see one of us dressed in fancy clothes, buckled shoes, and a powdered wig and made to parade the streets, holding a parasol with which to shade his mistress. I would rather have been a miserable field slave than a pet nigger.

"What do you say to that, Mr. Long?"

I admit with shame that I answered the good man with an ignoble caricature of the darky. I might have just stepped off a minstrel stage or from the cover of "Jump Jim Crow," adorned with a sketch of "Daddy" Rice blacked up and shuffling.

"No, suh," I said like the white man's idea of a coon. "I ain't interested."

I almost did a comical jig, but decided against it. The negro's self-caricature must never be obvious, or the white man will know that he is being mocked.

Emerson looked as if he could lynch me from the gas bracket. Garrison was embarrassed. Having stepped in a dung heap, I was eager to get away by myself, where the reek could not shame me even more.

"I's got be goin'," I said, and I left hastily, leaving those two champions of my people's cause to despise me.

In those days, even simple human transactions were complicated for me by doubt and self-loathing. I had let myself become the very thing I despised, and, in doing so, had abased myself before two men whose regard I valued. I was like a child who, having been caught in a lie, tells an even more outrageous one. A slave is ruled by three all-consuming emotions: fear, sorrow, and hatred. Ambivalence is a luxury of the freeborn. There were slaves, and there were masters. As one of the former, I had expected nothing, wished for nothing, hoped for nothing, aspired to nothing, been nothing but what I was. The way was clear, even though it led nowhere.

In the morning, a boy delivered a note from Emerson, asking if I would "please visit me at Bush, when convenient."

I knew that rancor could be concealed beneath a pleasing manner. Politeness was the perfect covert from which to shoot one's poisoned arrows. My impulse was to run and hide. I could make my way into Canada and, in its wilderness, lose myself. I might become a fur trapper. I had heard that the *coureurs des bois*, French-Canadian woodsmen, did not despise black people. But I was unprepared for such a life and for the quick death that would surely follow, with nothing to survive my frozen bones buried under snow but *The Florist's Guide* given to me by a Quaker woman.

Having resigned myself to Emerson's displeasure, I went to visit him that afternoon.

LIDIAN SHOWED ME INTO her husband's study. He had always been cordial, but this afternoon he did not rise to greet me. Unable to hold his gaze, I studied the steel pen on his desk, which had recently replaced his quill. Henry, too, had taken to using one, his a gift from Elizabeth Hoar on the occasion of his having left Concord for Staten Island to tutor Emerson's nephews. That job came to naught. The world meant Concord for Henry, and he could not leave it for long. I felt my face begin to burn under Emerson's gaze like a dry leaf kindled by sunlight through a glass. My refusal to face him squarely infuriated him as much as did the minstrelsy I had made of my meeting with Garrison. Magnanimous in his praise of others, Emerson had no doubt spoken well of me to the antislavery crusader. Knowing how much I had disappointed him made me all the more sullen and determined to prove myself unworthy of his friendship.

"Yesterday, you insulted the divinity within you," said Emerson at last. He spoke calmly and judiciously, but death warrants have been just as politely served.

"Divinity?" I repeated. The idea astonished and disturbed me.

"Yes," he said. "It is in each one of us."

In Jeroboam? I said to myself. In the slave catchers, man hunters, and nigger-breakers.

"I don't give a damn for it!" I said, finding courage to be rude. "I'd be much happier finding the *man* inside me. I'm not sure I have ever met him. It's he who interests me. You, Henry, and Mr. Garrison—what is it you want of me?"

"Your advancement."

Were we always to be treated like children?

"I want to be more than a well-spoken negro!" I cried, recalling the words I had uttered to myself in Freemasons' Hall. "I want to be more than a fancy nigger you can show off like a trick pony!"

My vehemence embarrassed him even more than the ugly word I had used—one that he strove to eliminate from the speech of his fellow New Englanders, if not from their minds, which were beyond his power to reform.

"I never intended to patronize you, and if I have done, I apologize. It is difficult to know how to approach another human being. Do you know what it means to be human, Samuel?"

I shook my head, for, at that moment, I did not know.

Later, I would recall the boy and the old man who had hidden me in the meadows near the James.

"Nor do I, although I have attempted to discover it and hope one day to do so."

Emerson looked up from his desk at me, his hands folded like a schoolboy's. He was waiting to hear what I would say. For the first time in my life, I had the upper hand. I stared at motes of dust dancing in a shaft of sunlight. I beheld my will as if it, too, were a shining thing. I admired it like a boy entranced by a bird's nest or a butterfly's wing. I could have made the man dance! Strange to say, however, I decided not to take advantage of him and his generous nature. I would neither play upon him, his feelings, nor play the fool for him. It was, I realized later on, a historic moment in my history. I had made the second-most important decision of my life: The first was having resolved to seek my freedom in the North. Emerson was still waiting for me to speak. I think he wanted my forgiveness. I wanted to ask for his but could not find the words.

"We are separated by a gulf." He was ill at ease, this man who seemed to have all words at his command. "One scarcely knows how to begin to cross it."

Ten years earlier, Emerson had written, "I think it cannot be maintained by any candid person that the African race have ever occupied or do promise to ever occupy any very high place in the human family." His views had changed since then, and only a few others, such as Garrison and the fugitive Douglass, could speak against slavery with his oratory, passion, and moral suasion. Emerson's compass had swung round to true north—to abolition. He had come a long way, if not so far as John Brown would travel by the time he reached Harper's Ferry.

He held out his hand, and I took it gladly. At that moment, I felt the absence of my left hand keenly and wondered what sign of reconciliation Emerson would have contrived if I had lacked the right one instead. The moment might have been all the more awkward for want of a conventional—a symbolical—gesture. Perhaps he would have embraced me, or possibly there would have been no reconciliation. We live suspended by filaments, deluding ourselves that we are upheld by our own cunning.

Outside in the yard, Lidian was repairing an old cucumber frame. Sunlight sparkled on the panes. Leaning over them, I saw my face and hers commingled there. Henry would have struck a rhetorical figure whose meaning would most likely have contained a morsel of truth.

"Have you and Mr. Emerson made it up between you?" asked Lidian.

I hoped he had not told her of my foolishness. Once again, I wondered about the private lives of public men, then shook off the thought as one does a pesky fly determined to settle on one's nose. I felt pity for this sickly woman with the haggard face. I sensed again a triumph in that pity.

"Let me do that, Mrs. Emerson."

"Thank you kindly, Mr. Samuel."

I was grateful that she had never once taken notice—by word or glance—of my handicap. She gazed at the tulip tree, its flowers rising like flames from among the leaves. There was no telling whether her satisfaction resided in the yellow blossoms only or—like that of her husband and the other Transcendentalists—comprehended the universe. Contented, she turned and left me to get on with my work.

The May sun fell warmly on me while I braced the joins, puttied the loose glazing, and scraped the scales from the wood, which I painted the green of the hull of Henry's old boat, the *Musketaquid,* renamed *Pond Lily* by Hawthorne. Perhaps the joy I took in that modest labor was what the Brook Farmers had felt at the beginning of their communal experiment, fated to come to grief, like most things that humankind attempts. But I would never find a job quite so satisfying as fixing Mrs. Emerson's cucumber frame.

The work had taken only half a mind; the balance swung about like a weathercock in a variable wind or a compass needle finding its way north, which, in my case, was Mr. Garrison and the discomfiture I had caused him. He deserved an apology, but I had not matured sufficiently to tender one. Besides, he had returned to Boston. I might have written a letter, but I could not trust myself to distill the rout of my emotions into sentences that would be understood without benefit of the author's gloss.

"Dear Sir: I apologize for my—"

What, exactly? My rudeness? Childish spite? My ignorance of good manners and, more to the point, of myself— the man I wished to be if only I could escape my cell like poor Edmond Dantès in *The Count of Monte Cristo*?

I will begin my atonement in Concord, I told myself. I will go and see Joseph.

I FOUND JOSEPH INSIDE the livery stable, currying "witches' stirrups" from the mane of a chestnut-colored horse.

"Afternoon, Samuel."

"Good afternoon," I replied with a sniff. A part of me still wanted to appear grand.

As if to explain his presence there, he said, "I help old Jake when his lumbago raises hell with him, if I have the time."

The horse shied, snorted, and stamped until Joseph calmed it with his hand.

"I heard you made a fool of yourself in front of Mr. Emerson and Mr. Garrison." The remark seemed innocent of criticism or ridicule, and I took it as such, trying all the while to ascertain whether or not he bore me a grudge.

"I did!" I said with a laugh, as if my contretemps had been a joke on them.

Honesty comes hard, even for an honest man, which I was not completely.

Joseph put down the currycomb, slapped the horse's rump affectionately, and closed the stall. He looked at me intently. What thoughts went through his mind, I could not have said. We went into the tackle room, where Jake had a deal table and a couple of chairs.

"Sit yourself, Samuel."

He took a bottle of corn whiskey from a liniment shelf, uncorked it, filled a glass, and set it in front of me.

"Drink," he said in a voice pitched somewhere between invitation and adjuration. "For Sunday's sake."

I enjoyed a glass of whiskey. But on the plantation, I had mostly resisted the temptation to get soused on the Sabbath with the other slaves, not out of prudery, but defiance. The masters encouraged inebriation on the Lord's Day in order to humiliate us and to discourage thoughts of running away. Six days we labored and, by nightfall, we were too worn-out to think; on the seventh day, those who might have been inclined to make trouble were stupefied by the *massa*'s liquor. Joseph seemed untroubled by reservations, unless he meant to test mine. I saw that he was studying me, taking my measure with the eye of a tailor or an undertaker. To refuse his whiskey might insult him. Possibly, he hoped to be insulted; it would give him cause to strike me or have done with me.

"Aren't you drinking, Joseph?"

"After you," he said quietly, nodding first at me and then at the glass. In the windowless room, his dark face was darker still. His eyes, what I could see of them, partook of the mystery of humankind, which is less comprehensible than that of the stars.

We were to drink from the common cup. Did he mean it to be a chalice of bitterness, or one of forgiveness? I swallowed some and felt the liquor's warmth. He drank off the rest and set the empty glass on the table as emphatically as a judge's gavel or an auctioneer's hammer. I could not see clearly the part I was to play in the melodrama he seemed to be making up as he went. I filled the glass again and drank until clarity grew overcast, as when the sun is hidden by clouds, trimming the brightness and erasing the shadows by which all things on earth are made distinguishable.

"I wasn't sure what kind of man you were," he said, wiping his lips on his sleeve.

It was the question I had been asking myself. I thought I knew the answer, but I could not have given it with whiskey fuddling my brain. Maybe I could not have answered him—drunk or sober. I would leave such ruminations to Emerson and the Transcendental Club.

"I'm like you," I said to Joseph, leaving it at that.

He must have interpreted my evasion to suit himself, because he became amiable.

"When I came east, I was like a wasp that's been smoked out of its nest," he said. "I was mad, and I wanted to sting— didn't matter who so long as they were white people."

Now, it was my turn to nod. I did so, I thought, with sagacity, as though I were R. W. Emerson himself. Being drunk, I might have looked foolish. Joseph had more to say, but I shut my ears to him. I listened to a wasp buzzing at the door to its house of ash-colored paper, built high up in the rafters. It was probably the very wasp—the *real* wasp—that had inspired Joseph's simile. Henry would have relished this moment, I said to myself, and hoped I would remember to tell him about it.

"Once I saw a dead boy in the pond," I said, apropos of nothing.

"You already said," muttered Joseph, who, by now, was also on the excursion boat that carries a man out onto the waters of oblivion, where the scenery is obscured by mist and a false memory of Eden. The world had turned golden like the whiskey.

I was ready to apologize to Garrison. I would put down the glass and walk the twenty miles to Boston. I would tell him the story of my life with the eloquence and credibility of Dickens relating Oliver Twist's. I would take Joseph with me so that he, too, could give an account of himself. Afterward, we would take a steamboat out onto the Atlantic and then head south to the Potomac and thence to Washington City, where we would address Congress. Our stories would so move its members that we would not have to demand or even ask for abolition. Those weak, contentious, backbiting men would become statesmen who, by acclamation, would put an end to human bondage. Everywhere, our people's chains would be struck off for all time.

And then I fell asleep.

I dreamed of riding to freedom inside a coffin, or maybe I did not dream but am only now recalling a vivid and harrowing thought that suddenly came to mind and seemed as doubtful as a dream.

In the morning, I woke to the nickering of a horse. In the stable, Joseph was reciting messianically from the Book of Exodus: "'And the Lord said unto Moses, Yet will I bring one plague more upon Pharaoh, and upon Egypt; afterwards he will let you go hence . . . And there shall be a great cry throughout all the land of Egypt, such as there was none like it, nor shall be like it any more.'" I was frightened, believing that Joseph had lost his wits in the night.

"Joseph, are you yourself this morning?"

My head pained me from the liquor and from having laid it all night on a sack of feed. I felt like somebody whose acquaintance I would not be pleased to make.

Joseph closed the book and looked into my eyes with a brightness and a fervor in his own that made me think again he had become deranged.

"I'm leaving Concord, and I want you to come with me."

"Where?"

"Mexico, Samuel. Soon, others of our race will join us there, and, when we're ready, we'll march—an army of negroes—into the South to free our people."

I looked at him as if he had just invited me to set myself afire or put a bullet in my brain.

"I've been thinking about this ever since I attended the Negro National Convention at Buffalo. I heard Henry Garnet's 'Call to Rebellion' and was stirred to the roots of my soul. We can't wait for enlightenment or for divine intervention to end our people's misery. We must do what is required of us now." He took a folded broadside from his pocket. "Listen, Samuel!"

He read from the broadside, which he had marked with a pencil manufactured by J. Thoreau & Co. Ironical, isn't it? Or maybe not: The Transcendentalists believe that all things are connected, which would preclude the idea of chance from the business of the universe. In any case, the Thoreaus made an excellent pencil, which Henry himself had perfected.

I have kept the broadside, and I will set down something of what Joseph read to me.

> You had far better all die—*die immediately*, than live slaves, and entail your wretchedness upon your posterity. If you would be free in this generation, here is your only hope. However much you and all of us may desire it, there is not much hope of redemption without the shedding of blood. If you must bleed, let it all come at once—rather, *die*

freemen, than live to be slaves. . . . Brethren, arise, arise! Strike for your lives and liberties. Now is the day and the hour. Let every slave throughout the land do this, and the days of slavery are numbered. You cannot be more oppressed than you have been—you cannot suffer greater cruelties than you have already. *Rather die freemen than live to be slaves.* . . . Let your motto be resistance! resistance! RESISTANCE! No oppressed people have ever secured their liberty without resistance. What kind of resistance you had better make, you must decide by the circumstances that surround you, and according to the suggestion of expediency. Brethren, adieu. Trust in the living God. Labor for the peace of the human race, and remember that you are FOUR MILLIONS.

Nathan Hale with a British noose around his neck must have looked as Joseph did then.

"I've been waiting for you, Samuel," he said, his eyes glinting with a light seen mostly in those of the insane or the possessed.

He was mad—yes, and perhaps he had always been.

"I am safe in Concord," I said, after having been momentarily returned to Jeroboam's stable by the bewitching odors of hay, manure, sweat, and leather.

"What is your safety against the continuing bondage of four million souls?"

I would not be swayed. A sane man does not put his head twice in the lion's mouth.

"You may have forgotten what it was like to be a slave," I said, "but I haven't."

I waved my wrist at him languidly, like someone refusing a beggar alms. Without a hand, the gesture must have appeared ridiculous. Had our situations been reversed, I would have laughed to see Joseph's empty cuff. His outrage increased to fury.

"It took courage to chop off your hand!" he cried. "Look into yourself to find it again."

"To lose a hand to a single chop was far easier for me to bear than the accrued pain of a thousand stripes. My back is a calendar of torment, every scar a week spent in hell. One more lash will finish me."

My histrionic remark must have sobered him. I watched his spine melt—that's how it seemed. His shoulders rounded, and his head lowered. He held on to a stall rail to keep from falling, or else from flying off like Elijah in the fiery chariot.

"Samuel, we have a moral duty to take up arms."

His indignation had blunted, and I began to wonder if I had allayed his brainstorm.

"Joseph, you are needed in Concord," I said cunningly.

He shook his head in doubt and sorrow.

"If I could kill all slavers, masters, overseers, drivers, and slave breakers with a thought, I would think it," I said. "But I can't, and I won't go back to 'Egypt' and the fiery furnace."

To have done so would have meant more than the whip, the spiked collar, or the inside of a barrel bristling with nails. I had caused willful and malicious damage to my master's property by having chopped off my hand. Of no further use to him, Jeroboam would hang me.

"I'll go alone, then," he said offhandedly, as if we had been arguing over a trip to Staten Island.

I was afraid, but I could not admit to my fear. Instead, I told him that I had work to do "on my character"; I needed to study the Word and see for myself whether or not He meant for me to spill blood.

"Take it." He thrust the broadside into my pocket. "It's the Word of God."

There is none so arrogant as a man with a righteous cause.

A few days after Joseph had wrestled with his angel, or devil, or, what is worse, himself, he left Concord. Whether he went to Mexico and marched against the South, with the Almighty at one side and Henry Garnet at the other, took passage to Africa, as Garnet had also urged, or died ingloriously in a crib, a knife worked between his ribs, I never heard.

I stayed inside my shanty, wishing I could remain, like Henry, aloof from politics and causes. I would have liked to tend beans, ponder, and play the flute to a mouse ensconced underneath the floorboards. I would have liked to sit on the front step in the evening and watch the pond turn transparent before taking on the gaudy colors of sunset. I would have liked to be a Romantic and peruse nature's book instead of Garrison's newspaper. I would like to have had a room at Bush, where I could have thought high-mindedly and fashioned toys for the Emersons' children.

Slavery is the first injustice, against which all other hardship and privation are mere annoyance; the drudgery of a purposeless life is the second. The first destroys the human spark and the body that should have housed it; the second, the mind, which Emerson says is holy. In those days, I read the Bible in search of the comfort one takes in the story of another's misery. I read *The Pilgrim's Progress* and thought Christian was a fool. I had lived too long in the City of Destruction to consider the Celestial City anything but a slave's daydream. Divine Providence might have embraced the sparrow, but not the negroes— nor the Indians, the Chinese, the Irish, or the Hebrews. God would cast an earthward gaze from heaven's tower and admire his roses, while the man hunters dragged me back to Virginia.

Emerson had asked me what it meant to be human. I should have told him that a person cannot be human if his life is perpetually in the grip of terror and uncertainty. Just as cities are built by people unafraid of marauding barbarians and the caprices of a hostile universe, so will we become human when we no longer live in fear for our lives.

FENDA WAS AN OLD WOMAN when I visited her. Her skin was the color of a coffee bean but not so smooth anymore. It was no longer read by her husband's fingers, affectionately or passionately, according to the blood's tides and fevers. Bright rags were twisted in her thin hair, giving her a fantastical appearance.

"I want to know what will happen to me," I said after a child had answered my knock and taken me inside to her.

In the dusky room, she sat with a ball of wool on her skirts, knitting like Fate a span of mortal life, and I found myself looking nervously at what wool remained before she must taper off and finish.

Not me, I prayed, and the voice inside my head was that of a child, sitting in the slave pen, waiting to be sold. Let it be somebody else's strand she works!

We are said to be a superstitious race. The kindest masters look upon us as benighted children in need of oversight; the cruelest consider us brutes incapable of reason and therefore beneath God's notice. The Quaker widow, who sent me northward from Brooklyn, had read me a poem of William Blake's that began:

> My mother bore me in the southern wild,
> And I am black, but O! my soul is white;
> White as an angel is the English child:
> But I am black as if bereav'd of light.

Blacks may be naïve, but so are poets who gaze wistfully at the world and hope to find large meanings in small things. They search for intimations with which to shake off the confines of a narrow life as avidly as any astrologer, medium, or diviner. Superstitions, myths, poems—what are they if not appeals against the death sentence handed down at the moment of our birth? They are proof of our fear and yearning. What were Henry's Walden Pond, Waldo's Over-Soul, and the Phalansteries of the associationists if not petitions to something beyond the tiny fires in the darkness that are every one of us?

Fenda laid her knitting in her lap and, at a glance, took my measure.

"I can see your past plain enough," she said.

"It's the future that interests me; I know my past," I said, trying not to sound flippant.

"Just because you've had one don't mean you know it," she replied placidly.

I sighed and was about to leave her to her mystifications, when she laughed.

"Mister," she said, "you are touchy as a white man!"

Maybe I was at that.

"What you want to know for?" she asked.

"Because I'm scared I won't have one."

"Everybody has their future to get through the best they can."

"I deserve a happy one!" I blurted.

"Nobody—man, woman, or little child—deserves anything except as God wills it."

At that moment, Fenda might have been the Almighty or one of the ferocious goddesses of the Hindus or the Babylonians. I would not have been surprised had she put on the head of a jackal or a robe of fire. Like a voodoo priestess, she could have tied her soul to the wool in her lap and bid it strangle me as the serpents had Laocoön and his sons.

"I'll tell you what you want to know," she said, relenting. Perhaps she saw my fear or smelled it. Her nostrils had flared. In any case, she spoke gently, almost sadly, now. "As much as I can know of it."

I thanked her more profusely than she deserved after having disconcerted me. She called to the child—her granddaughter—to bring a bowl of cool water, a candle, and a phosphorus match. I watched while she lit the candle, mumbled words to herself, and let the melted tallow drip into the bowl, where it made shapes on the water. Fenda then took up the bowl and brought it close to her clouded eyes.

"I sees a body falling in the water," she said simply.

I supposed she meant the Carlson boy.

"I sees a book, but I don't see your name wrote on its pages."

I supposed it was one that Henry was writing.

"What else," I asked impatiently.

"Piles of dead men."

That, in itself, was not an uncommon sight.

"What killed them?" I asked.

She shook her head. Whether she was old or cataracts had also grown over her second sight, she saw nothing of the coming war between North and South, with its staggering heaps of corpses. She did not see Bull Run or Shiloh in the wax shapes floating in the bowl or the death of Henry's friend John Brown.

She scattered barley onto a flat stone and scried what might befall me in the pattern of the grains.

"Will I love a woman?"

"You will 'know' a woman but not love," she replied.

"Where? Where will I 'know' her?"

"In Adam's Woods."

"When?"

"Don't know," she said, sweeping barley grains from the stone with the edge of her hand. Her fingers, I saw, were gnarled like pine branches.

Seeing my disappointment with whatever vision of the

outer world remained to her, she smiled ruefully, and, with a shrug of her frail shoulders, which I could easily have mistaken for a tremor, she said she was sorry.

Was she sorry for my unhappy future, or did she regret that she could be of little help to me in meeting it? I did not ask. I put a few coins in her hand—inscribed with an unintelligible future of its own—and left her. I stood in the dooryard, listening to the *click, click, click* of her needles.

III

A week after Joseph's fiery departure, I was sitting beside Hawthorne in a car of the Fitchburg Railway. Having been in Concord, he was traveling to Boston to meet with his publisher, William Ticknor, and celebrate publication of his new book, *Mosses from an Old Manse*. Emerson had suggested that I accompany Hawthorne to Boston so that I could see to my own business there. He had gone so far as to buy my ticket and provide me with enough money for meals and a night's stay in the town.

Also enclosed in the envelope was the briefest of notes: "Give my regards to Mr. Garrison." I was annoyed by Emerson's presumption—but only slightly. I had intended to apologize to the abolitionist, and Emerson had merely supplied the means to that end.

That morning on the train to Boston, I was besotted by movement. Mistress Jeroboam had once invited me to peer through a phenakistoscope. It amused her to see the dismay of her house niggers when they beheld, for the first time, the illusion of a horse set in frantic motion by the turning of a crank. In the same way, the world outside the carriage window appeared to dissolve to eyes innocent of speed. I had never before traveled more rapidly than a wagon or steamboat allowed. I glanced at Hawthorne—admired for his darkly handsome looks—to see what effect our headlong progress was having on him. He appeared not to notice, his hazel eyes fixed on the page of a book.

The fields flashed green or brown, according to their cultivation; ditches, brimming with recent rain, shone or turned black as clouds shambled past the sun; and telegraph poles—like an endless row of crosses—lurched behind us into a cloud of coal smoke. Having tired of reading, Hawthorne closed his book, stretched his legs in the aisle, and smiled.

"The first time aboard a train is thrilling."

I agreed.

"I do miss Concord," he said. "It suited me."

I gave him a practiced look suggestive of polite inquiry.

"I am not comfortable in society and was under less obligation than I am in Salem or Boston. I don't dislike people, but I tend to be shy of them." He was silent awhile and then said, "Concord is dangerous, however; it can do mischief to those of weaker intellect."

"How so?" I asked, his last remark having taken me by surprise.

"Idealism scares me, Samuel."

Idealism meant nothing to me. I was sick of philosophy and wished that I might turn my head to the window and continue my observation of the earth in motion. I was fascinated, as if I were seeing the planet itself turning on its axis and hearing, in the train's lumbering, the groan of its iron hinge.

"Emerson's world consists of sublimely radiant ideas far removed from the lives of mill girls in Lowell, shoemakers in Lynn, hands in the lead-pipe works in Concord—or from those who like to drink their beer in Bigelow's taproom. Waldo has a puritanical streak in him, and, like most ascetics, he doesn't much care for our fallen world."

I gave every appearance of being interested in what he had to say, although my mind was becoming lulled by the clicking of the tracks.

"He mistrusts our animal nature, and *I* have every reason to fear Puritanism," he said. "My great-great-grandfather was a judge at the witch trials of the 1690s and never repented of it. It was a short step from Plymouth Rock, on which *his* father had stood, to the Salem pillory and stake. I've always feared that a strain of intolerance, which is no more than an extra measure of devotion to an ideal, might be a part of my character that needs only to be 'barked' for the grain to show."

He murmured like a fly trapped in a jam pot. The light passed through my closed lids—pink and wavering, turning black when the train entered a grove of thickset trees. Words fell like meteors through a twilight of sleep: "Fanatical ... theocracy ... skepticism ... arbiter ... reason ... mischief ... ecstasy ... sin ..." I saw Henry on the river, sitting in the green-and-blue boat, waving his soft hat toward me and shouting, "Samuel! Samuel! Samuel, we're here."

Hawthorne was nudging me good-naturedly.

"I'm afraid my dull oratory put you to sleep."

"I heard some," I replied, as the world reemerged from somnolence.

"A bad speech, like a glass of raw whiskey, is best appreciated at its finish, when the senses are addled and judgment is in abeyance."

Emerson, Hawthorne, Thoreau, who, of the three, had the least concern for his reputation, could mint sentences bright as new pennies. They could have filled almanacs with their clever turns. Listening to them in conversation—Emerson leading, Thoreau affirming or contradicting, Hawthorne by turns romantic, mute, and ironical—I would become lost like Hansel and Gretel in the woods—scattered crumbs eaten by birds—or like Hester Prynne and Arthur Dimmesdale in theirs—goodness eaten away by sin and spite. All three men spoke to posterity. They were concerned with a future in which I had no place. Each one viewed the world through a separate curtain—lace, cretonne, or burlap redolent of dust. At the time, I believed that, of the four of us, only I saw the world for what it was: a plantation writ large. Emerson's Nature, Henry's Walden, Hawthorne's Puritans were nothing but stories. I believed then that stories did not contain even so much as a morsel of truth, nor were they intended to unravel a mystery. They themselves were mysteries—insolvable and useless. I wonder if I do not believe that even now.

Hawthorne and I left the depot. Outside on Kneeland Street, Boston thrust up all around us, brick and stone, elm and chestnut trees, while down in the harbor, masts of sailing ships stood stiffly against the sky.

"I'll leave you to your own affairs, then," said Hawthorne,

patting the top of his high hat to secure it against a freshening breeze that brought the smell of salt and tar from the east, where the bay and ocean were. "Do you know how to reach your destination?"

I could not decide if he knew I was bound for *The Liberator* offices. I told him I would find my way and left it at that.

"We'll meet at Lamb Tavern, at Three Sixty-nine Washington Street." He turned me toward the north and said, "Walk up Lincoln to Summer Street, then head northeasterly to Washington. I'll be there at five o'clock. We're staying the night at Park House, near the Common. We'll be quite comfortable, and the cost is reasonable."

I nodded. He smiled once again and was soon gone around a corner. I was proud that he had tipped his beaver hat to me, and I looked to see if anyone had noticed.

I asked a cabman if he knew the way to Garrison's newspaper.

"Are you riding or going by shank's mare?" he asked suspiciously, taking his pipe from between his bearded lips.

"I'm afraid I must walk," I said, turning out my pockets to prove my lack of means. I had hidden Emerson's largesse inside my shoe. The cabman, aloof on his seat, was not inclined to be helpful now that the possibility of a fare had been scotched.

"I'd very much appreciate the kindness, sir." I hated that "sir."

"Oh, very well!" he grumbled. He thumbed a dog-eared copy of *Stimpson's Boston Directory* till he came to the newspaper's address. "Twenty-five Cornhill."

"I'm much obliged to you, sir."

I knew better than to ask the way. He returned to smoking his church warden, and I went on until I saw a policeman, who gruffly directed me. The newspaper occupied the first floor of a brick building distinguished from a street of uniformly cheerless commercial enterprises by its signboard bearing the newspaper's name and motto: *The Liberator. Our Country Is the World—Our Countrymen Are Mankind.* Standing at the street door, I felt my nerve—strained by each step I had taken after having left Hawthorne—failing.

What was I but an insolent fool to have insulted a man like Garrison, whose infamy was proof of his sincerity toward the great cause he espoused. I recalled stories of his courage that Henry had told me during our rambles. Accused of having fomented Nat Turner's grisly revolt, the Georgia Senate had put a five-thousand-dollar bounty on his head. He had been burned in effigy in Charleston and condemned from pulpits even in his native Boston, where a gallows had been raised outside his house. In 1835, during an address to the Boston Female Anti-Slavery Society, the hall had been stormed. Garrison escaped through a window but was seized by the mob, dragged through the streets, and, a noose having been put around his neck, he would have been lynched had it not been for the sheriff who jailed him. I could not do otherwise than admit that William Garrison was a braver man than I and risked more for abolition than Emerson, who argued, however cogently, for emancipation from the safety of lecture platforms and journal pages.

I got up nerve at last and went inside, where I was greeted by a young man whose shirt sleeves were engulfed by enormous sleeve protectors spotted with ink. My entrance had made him pause in his flight toward what I assumed was the press, whose mechanical clatter I could hear nearby. He wore a galley draped over one arm like a waiter's linen cloth. Impatient to be gone about his business, he spoke to me nevertheless with the utmost respect—even, I thought, admiration. For an instant, I imagined that I saw in his face something very like envy, but such could not have been the case.

"May I assist you in anything, sir?" he asked.

"I wish to see Mr. Garrison, if convenient. I have come from Concord for the purpose."

"May I tell Mr. Garrison your name?"

"Mr. Samuel Long."

On hearing my name, did I imagine that he frowned?

"If you'll please take a seat, I'll tell him you are here."

He withdrew down the hall. He seemed to be gone longer than was necessary. I began to fidget on the hard wooden chair while the clock over my head ticked off the seconds. The sharp smell of printer's ink and dust stung my nose. Perhaps, I thought, I am to be kept waiting as a chastisement for my affront to Garrison and the cause. Then the door at the end of the passage opened, and Garrison came toward me.

"Mr. Long," he said without much warmth. "You wish to see me?"

He was civil, if reserved. I did not merit a friendly reception.

"I have something to say to you, if you'll allow me."

"Very well. We can speak privately in my office."

I followed him into an office cramped by an accumulation of books, pamphlets, and paper that spilled everywhere like excelsior from a broken crate. There was no prim green desk as in Henry's cottage, nor an impressive one announcing a scholar of importance as in Emerson's virtuously plain study. Garrison's was the office of a busy man who had, in Hawthorne's words, "work to do in the world."

I glanced outside the window, where an enormous cask seemed to be floating down the street like a Spanish galleon. I had once traveled in just such a vessel. At the curb, a man was beating a dray horse, which hung its head dispiritedly. Garrison cleared his throat. I turned and sought his eyes, determined not to let my gaze wander. He searched mine with the watery eyes of someone who has spent his life poring over pages of printed matter. He was small, narrow, and worn, with a head nearly as bald and seemingly as breakable as an egg. I wondered all the more that such a man should be so very *much* a man that he could ignore the threat of a public humiliation and a repulsive death such as is usually reserved for people of color.

"Mr. Garrison," I said, "I wish to apologize for my discourtesy to you at the Lyceum in Concord."

"I was appalled by your hateful caricature of the negro," he said in the sternest of voices.

He was angry, and I saw the fearlessness and probity of a man who could defy a lynch mob. Before my eyes, he seemed to grow in stature. To all appearances a grammar school master or a grocer's assistant, he became, in my fancy, an Old Testament prophet—an Ezekiel in spectacles, foretelling the destruction of Jerusalem. I could have bowed down to him, but he would have mistaken my awe for abasement—more of the "hateful caricature."

"Did you intend to shame your people by it?"

"No," I said, rising to my full height to show him that I was unbowed. I, too, wanted to appear fearless.

Abruptly, his manner changed toward me. Where, a moment before, light had flashed angrily from the twin panes of his spectacles, now I could see kindness—sadness—in his eyes.

"Can you tell me, Mr. Long, what possessed you to ape Brother Tambo? To play the fool—a 'darky' or a 'coon' in a 'Tom show'?"

I was like the animal inside the oyster shell: naked and vulnerable. Fancifully speaking, I wanted to shut the doors to my shell on their hinges and waggle my muscular tongue down into the mud to hide myself from Garrison's piercing gaze.

"I doubted your sincerity," I said after a silence.

"How so?" My remark had clearly taken him by surprise.

"I believed your interest in me went only as far as I could be useful to you. I was a knife you could sharpen on the grindstone of your righteousness," I said like a well-spoken negro.

"Would that not be a good thing?" he asked.

I heard the creak of shoe leather as he shifted his weight from one foot to the other.

"No matter how righteous the cause, I don't want to be useful at the price of being used. I'm sick of people's curiosity. I am sick of being a curiosity."

Now it was my turn to be surprised by his magnanimity. He stood behind his chair and inclined his head toward me, saying, "Then it is I who must apologize."

For me to have rebuffed him—for reasons self-evident or obscure—would have been churlish.

"I'll be glad to tell you my story," I said.

He nodded, and I saw he meant to make no more of the folly that had brought me to his office. He called to the young man who had admitted me.

"Mr. Owens," he said when the man appeared in the doorway. "Mr. Long has consented to share his story with our readers. Will you be so kind as to take down his words?"

"Yes, sir," he said, sitting at a corner of Garrison's desk with pencil and foolscap at the ready.

Garrison motioned that I, too, should sit and then did so himself.

"In your own time, Mr. Long, and in your own way," said Garrison, cleaning the glass of his much-smudged spectacles with a handkerchief, into which, having finished his polishing, he blew his nose.

Haltingly, I narrated the events that time had spun into the thread of my life, in the order of their imperfect recollection. I appeared to be looking at Garrison, but what I saw were scenes from the past, translucent, like magic lantern slides. The result of my maundering later appeared in *The Liberator*. I will copy into this, my eulogy for Henry, passages from the published account having to do with my flight to freedom—what there can be of it for a fugitive. I have said enough already about my preceding years as a slave.

A SLAVE NARRATIVE:
AS TOLD BY SAMUEL LONG TO WILLIAM LLOYD GARRISON

. . . When I had staunched the blood issuing from the stump of my wrist with hot tar, I walked through the vegetable patch as slowly as I dared, so as not to attract attention. Seen at a distance, I would have appeared like any other slave, and I'd had the presence of mind to put a hoe over my shoulder to further the deception. I made my way across a field planted with corn and managed to enter the woods at the back of Mr. Jeroboam's plantation. Beyond it was a creek overgrown with sumac and cottonwood trees. My intention was to conceal myself in a thicket near the water, where I could quench my thirst and rest awhile. I was fortunate in having fresh water close to hand and also in its being late in the day, an hour or two until the sun would begin to set. I do not believe that, had I made my escape earlier in the day, I could have gotten away. Furthermore, if there had been no convenient woods, I would have soon been seized. Not caring for the hunt like his neighbors, Mr. Jeroboam did not keep dogs, another fact in my favor; dogs, especially bloodhounds, are more dangerous to a man in flight for his life than are men, who, unless they be Red Indians, can more readily be outwitted or "thrown off the scent."

I slept until dark, or nearly, when I roused myself and went stealthily through the woods which, now that night had fallen, were blacker even than the moonless sky. Leaving them, I was careful to make certain no one was by the creek—called Ballard Creek—or in the narrow marsh between it and the trees. I waded into the water and, aided by the dead limb of a tree, let the current carry me downstream to Ragged Creek, a journey of not more than five miles. There I hid on one of the small pine-covered islands in the brackish marsh on the south bank of the James.

I lived on oysters, which were plentiful—their meat, a delicious buttery flavor—and clean water from a spring. I suffered neither hunger nor thirst, although I was very much afraid. Sometimes I could hear the baying of dogs, but if they had been set on me, they would be sure to have lost my scent where I had entered the creek. All the while I was on the island—six or seven days—I saw only a boy carrying an old fowling piece, going in search of ducks, and an old man pulling up sweet-flag root, an Indian remedy for fever and troubles of the stomach. If I suffered hardship, it was the clouds of mosquitoes and black-flies that hovered above the creek and marshland, especially at night. They drew blood and raised welts on my bare chest and arms. I had escaped from the stable wearing just my cotton pantaloons. Only my back was proof against the pests because of its scars, which had been laid down through the years with the patience of a woman at her needle. I thought I'd go mad with the incessant itch and the persistent buzz of flies and sizzle of mosquitoes, the clamor of marsh birds.

I don't know when I came down with fever. I might have cured myself with sweet-flag tea, but I had no matches and would have been scared to light a fire if I'd had some. I could not get warm, though the days and nights were mild. I shook and my teeth chattered for what seemed like days, as I lay on a bed of pine boughs. I had dreams of— I couldn't have said what. They were strange and broken. I bit down on a stick to keep myself from crying out. Awake, I felt no better.

Everything around me appeared to tilt, as though I had drunk too much corn liquor. My brain felt salted—scooped out and put in brine. I had a most terrible thirst. The stink of dank mud and rotting shellfish became intolerable, making me retch. I tasted blood from the bit that had been in my mouth. I lay there without a thought for my safety—not trusting in the Almighty or in providence, for I hadn't wits enough to trust or think or keep myself from harm. I was no better than an insensate thing—a rotting log, a cottonwood stump, a dead bird. I might have been eaten by water rats, stung by snakes, or discovered by a man hunter. But no harm befell me during that time of travail, and I thank God or providence for it.

I said that I might have been discovered by a man hunter—or a citizen of Isle of White County, Virginia, convinced that a runaway ought to be returned to his master, according to the laws of Virginia and of God, who gave the white race dominion over the black one. Instead, it was the old man, who had been after sweet-flag roots, who found me and, with his son, carried me—not to safety, for there was none for a fugitive and his abettors, but to his nearby farm. We went at night like thieves. I will not give the names of my benefactors, in case they should become known and punished for their good deeds.

I stayed in their house, sleeping in a narrow chamber hidden behind a wall. Its rough lathwork coated with plaster and horsehair reminded me of Bucephalus and the stable from which I had made my reckless escape. The old man and his son fed me broth, gave me sweet-flag and burdock teas, cared for my wound, and brought me back to health and strength.

"Why do you put yourselves in jeopardy?" I asked them one night. I was sitting in a corner of their parlor, out of sight of anyone who might have peered through the window—the glazing changed by night and candlelight into a mirror. In it, I could see the reflection of the old man's face, gilded by firelight. "For a stranger, a runaway black man?"

They replied, at first, with a silence lengthy and deep enough for me to hear a candlewick sputter in the sconce, a pine branch crackle on the grate, the dog scratch an itch with its hind leg. The son yawned onto the back of his hand and then wiped his lips with it, as though the question had been answered long before now and could no longer worry him. For the space of that silence, the world might have been changed—slavery abolished, evil men reformed, Jesus resurrected, and the New Jerusalem established.

And then the father said, "'But why dost thou judge thy brother? or why dost thou set at nought thy brother? for we shall all stand before the judgment seat of Christ.'"

I thought I heard his son make some small affirming noise, but perhaps it was only the house that I had heard, sighing out its contentment up in the rooftree. In any case, no more was said by them on the subject of obligation. I would think of those two men—whose virtue might have been crumbs inside the pockets of their coats for all they made of it—when Emerson asked me later what it meant to be human.

After several days had passed without misadventure or alarm, the son took me the half mile across the James in a canoe. We traveled by night, encouraged by a heavy mist that had settled on the marshland and the broad river, and landed on the far shore at Warwick, the old county seat. His father had provided me with clothes appropriate to the station of freedman, in addition to five dollars and a letter, written on good paper in a fussy hand, purporting to be an offer of employment from a draper's establishment in Baltimore. A second letter, giving every appearance of age and handling, attested to my freeborn status. At a glance, it would allay suspicions if I were forced into the open—there to rely on my own wits.

We the Subscribers do certify that Samuel Long, a negro man, lived when a boy with Thomas Armatt in Richmond. When Mr. Armatt moved to Philadelphia, Long lived with John Cadwalder. We have always understood that he was born free and as a free man he has lived many years in this county of Warwick, in Virginia.

Oct. 7, 1834   John Littlejohn
                                               Jacob Murrey

In Warwick Towne, my next "conductor" was a cooper. Without delay, he bid me climb into a large oak cask, where I was promptly sealed up. The alacrity with which I found myself plunged into utter darkness dismayed me, but I was encouraged by a provision of johnnycake, a flask of water, and one of wine to fortify me on my journey. The cask was soon hoisted onto a wagon, and a team of horses toiled along roads that were, by turns, rough and stony, corduroyed, and cobblestoned. I would remain inside the cask for several days, nibbling johnnycake and taking water sparingly. I had had experience of close confinement in what Mr. Jeroboam called the "little ease," a cramped prison in which one could neither lie down at full length nor stand, and I was only slightly incommoded inside the cask, which was destined for a brewery in the North. Had its eventual contents been bourbon instead of beer, the interior would have been charred to flavor and color it. Fortunately, I was spared the irony and the soot.

In time, the wagon stopped, and from the noise of capstans, winches, gulls, and caulking hammers, I surmised that we had reached a port town. After a while, the cask was taken off the wagon and set in what I assumed was a warehouse or a shed near the water, whose dank odor reached me through the bunghole in the cask. I could hear the shouts of stevedores, draymen, and porters in the distance. Once, I overheard two men talking; they must have been standing just outside the cask. I held my breath, afraid they would discover me.

"He's a bastard, that one."

"He's that, and no denying it."

"I'd like to stick my hook in him."

"I wouldn't care if you did."

"Will you go to Denis Kelly's place tonight?"

"Oh, I should think so."

One of the men patted the swelling side of the cask affectionately. He would have dragged me out and put his hook in *me* if he had known I was lurking inside. "I could drink this dry," he said.

"It's a grand thing to—"

They walked off, and I could breathe easier once again.

I slept poorly that night—I assumed it was night because of the silence into which the world seemed to have fallen, disturbed fitfully by the creak of lapstrake planking and straining hawsers. By now, the air inside the cask was foul, despite the missing plug in the bunghole, through which I was able to draw breath and save myself from a faint. The smell of oak, ordinarily pleasing, sickened me, and I longed for the tang of salt water carried on a freshening wind. I attempted to distract myself with imagining what life in the North would be like for me, but I could picture little more than a street down which negroes walked in fine clothes.

In the morning, announced by the resumption of sounds peculiar to wharves, the cask was hauled—on a kind of trolley, I supposed—onto the pier, swung aloft, and let down into a cargo hold. I kept silent vigil over the dark and by now familiar mysteries of the cask, which I had come to think of as my casket. I reminded myself of the terrors and privations of the Middle Passage. What was my cramped journey next to *that?* In two days' time, the schooner, whose name I later learned was *Grace*—as though I had been a person in Bunyan's allegory—entered Lower New York Bay at Sandy Hook and sailed through the Narrows to New York. At last, the cask was raised from the hold, put onto another wagon, and carried along a noisy street. My dulled senses awoke to the screech of the barrel head being prized off by an iron crowbar. In a moment, I was staggering on unsteady legs, my eyes black and stinging in the weak light that fell through the dirty panes set in the warehouse roof.

"What place is this?" I asked stupidly. At that moment—so rich with possibility—I had not an inkling of my whereabouts.

"Chambers Street Warehouse," said the man who had freed me like Jonah from the belly of the whale. "That's the North River, which some call the Hudson," he said, motioning toward a nearby river—what I could see of it sparkling between the masts of numerous ships docked at the bottom of the street.

I must have appeared bewildered, because the man—a teamster wearing a leather apron and cap—exclaimed, "New York City, north of the Battery!"

His irritation frightened me, and I handed him my forged papers, as I would have to any white man in authority.

"Nothing to do with me," he said, handing them back. He must have regretted his harsh tone. I saw pity in his stubbled face, and clung—shamefully—to it. I almost wished that he would pat me on the head the way Mr. Jeroboam sometimes did when he was feeling well disposed toward his negroes. He would repent of his weakness—he considered it so—and the next day, he would repudiate his human feeling with the lash. "You're a free man," the teamster said, "though if I were you, friend, I'd waste no time in getting farther north. Man hunters are on the prowl, in search of runaways."

He had called me "friend"!

He gave me a suit of "Sunday" clothes, done up in brown paper and string. In a pocket of the frock coat was the address of a lady living in Brooklyn. The "conductors" deserve hosannas and trumpets for their bravery, but they would suffer for their glory. In any case, they are of a type of men and women that does not seek acknowledgment for the good they do.

I left the warehouse timidly, like a dog that had been kept a long while in a cage. I had never before seen so many people in one place. The streets were loud with shouting and the neighing of horses, of wagons clattering over cobblestones, and the ceaseless to-and-fro of all manner of people. All was a whirl, as though I were viewing the world through Mistress Jeroboam's phenakistoscope.

I walked across the lower part of Manhattan, until I came to a ferry slip on the East River. Shops and manufactories jammed the streets. Not even in Richmond, where Jeroboam had bought me, had I seen so many people crowding, jostling, and speaking in all the tongues of Babel. The sky here seemed far away, and I felt lonelier than I had on Ragged Island, or inside the cask—the final instrument of my deliverance. I began to shake as I had in the marsh while stricken with fever. Why had I come? I asked myself. What business can I possibly have here?

I boarded a ferry and made myself small in the stern amid crates and hampers of peevish chickens and hissing geese. Their clamor was answered by my own uproarious heart and by the mechanical clatter of steamboats. Black rags of coal smoke unraveled from iron stacks of packet boats, ferries, and side-wheelers crisscrossing the river. The river was brown, fast, and rolling; it made not the slightest impression of softness the way some rivers do. Instead, it made me think of rust and sheets of cold corrugated iron; I could feel its undulations underfoot.

Having docked on the opposite shore of the East River, I soon found myself at the address in Brooklyn Heights that had been given to me. I cannot be more explicit for the good woman's sake. She was of middle age, and, by her clothes, bonnet, and quaint speech, I took her for a Quaker. She did not ask me about my life. Having just escaped bondage, I had none yet that I could call mine. I was satisfied to watch her ply the needle, read the newspaper, look down the heights at the river, and cosset a kitten, which her son had given her to lessen her loneliness. She was, she told me without self-pity, recently widowed. She practiced what the Friends call an "expectant waiting upon God." Her house was plain, like her dress and speech. I stayed there for a day and a night. Of my brief time with her, I remember a bowl of gillyflowers, vivid and colorful—even garish amid the austere furnishings. They made me homesick. Can you imagine anything more unfathomable than the human heart?

I left that peaceable kingdom on the heights above the river early in the morning with pocket money, a loaf of unleavened bread such as the fugitive Israelites took with them into Canaan, and a small book my benefactress gave me to read during the last leg of my journey: *The Florist's Guide*, by T. Bridgeman, gardener, seedsman, and florist, published in New York. I have enjoyed that little work through the years for its homely enthusiasm and observations quite in keeping with Henry's and Emerson's own. I recall this verse in particular:

> Thine is a glorious volume, Nature! Each
> Line, leaf, and page, is fill'd with living lore;
> Wisdom more pure than sage could ever teach,
> And all philosophy's divinest store;
> Rich lessons rise where'er thy tracks are trod:
> The book of Nature is the book of God.

At the Catherine Street slip, I boarded a packet boat and watched as the Brooklyn Navy Yard at Wallabout Bay fell into the hazy distance, the reach behind us churned by our stern paddle. We traveled the East River's tidal strait past Bushwick Inlet, Newtown, and Newtown Creek, which divides Brooklyn and Queens. With the finger of Blackwell's Island to larboard, we steamed through Hell Gate and, at Throggs Neck, we entered Long Island Sound.

I would have been ignorant of our northerly progress if it had not been for an affable "traveler in furbelows," as a fellow passenger said after having introduced himself. He was dressed

like most who drum for business, and he had with him the
usual cases of the commercial trade.

"Mine," he said with a wink, "are not much heavier than a
drawerful of ladies' pantalets."

Ordinarily, I would have shied from a man careless of his
words, whose meaning tended to be broad, even vulgar. A slave
must be guarded in his speech—silence, in fact, is the safest way
to escape the rod. The drummer's casual manner disquieted me.
I might offend him by my reserve or by too great a familiarity.
When he offered me a drink from the pint bottle of rye he kept
in his pocket, I hesitated. Finally, I drank to his good health,
careful not to wipe the bottle's lip on my sleeve. I was glad
when the conversation—it was more like a monologue—returned
to the geography through which the boat was slowly passing,
clouds of coal smoke billowing from the stacks.

"You can see Brown Hills," he said, pointing with his stick
southeasterly across the sound. "They seem almost to jump up
out of the water at Orient, on the North Fork of Long Island."
He continued his enumeration. "Ahead is Plum Island and then
Fishers Island, like a fish bone stuck in the throat of Block
Island Sound. We'll steam past New Shoreham . . . Falmouth,
on Vineyard Sound . . . Clay Cliffs . . . Aquinnah Cliffs . . .
Nauset Beach . . . Truro . . . and Provincetown, where we'll
strike northwesterly for Boston Light."

I watched crazed gulls hunt the white furrows of our wake as
robins do earthworms after rain. The whole world is born with
a hunger, I thought. We spend our lives in trying to appease it.

"We should arrive in Boston harbor in two days' time,"
said the traveler in furbelows, "provided the weather, the Atlantic, and the god of steam raise no serious objections." He
spat over the side in the direction of the wind and said,

"Always spit to leeward, never to windward"—as good a piece of advice as any I have heard.

He had traveled many times on the Boston packet in pursuit of commercial buyers for his "dainties," and knew the lay of the land. Eventually, I grew tired of his asides on the cities and towns, hotels and oyster bars between Yonkers and Commercial Street in Boston. Apologizing for deserting him at the larboard rail, which he seemed reluctant to leave, I went below into a makeshift steerage, where benches and hammocks had been provided for common travelers. My eyes ached from having stared for so long across the water, whose salt had burned my wind-chafed lips. Feeling unwell, I lay on one of the benches, afraid of presuming to occupy a hammock. I slept but saw no dreamy coastal towns pass in review while the boat headed north.

I came up from the black waters of sleep, like one who is drowning, to find beefy hands around my throat. Lungs near to bursting, I struggled to draw breath, fearing that my windpipe would be crushed. Abruptly, a man removed his hands from my neck. The air rasped as I took it in with the avidity of a man at his last gasp.

"Benches are for sitting!" he snarled. I could smell liquor and onions on his breath. "Only a dumb nigger would sleep on a bench."

His face swung in and out of darkness—or rather, the light on his face did as the oil lamp suspended overhead swung back and forth like the tongue of a bell. I thought of a bell because one was ringing the hour up on deck. I hadn't the presence of mind to count the strokes.

"I'm sorry, sir," I said with a resentment I would not have felt when a slave, any more than a pig could resent its sty or a monkey its cage. Bondman, pig, and monkey can fear, hate, and suffer their squalid confinement, but resentment requires a luxury of time and subtlety of thought denied to animals and brutalized human beings. I hated this white man, a choleric drunkard who was no better than a slave breaker or a man hunter. I felt my neck tenderly, as if to assure myself that there was no rope around it.

"I gag on the smell of you coloreds! If you know what's good, you'll get up on deck and air yourself out."

I ought to have risen up in fury. The moment demanded it; my story, which was unspooling the thread God had given me, demanded it. It was the point to which all my life seemed to have been tending. But to what purpose my righteous indignation? The man could easily have finished me and left me for dead amid crates of geese, their gristly necks destined for the meeting of the ax and the block. I had traveled too far to be murdered by an enraged bigot on the packet to Boston. I am no Frederick Douglass or Harriet Tubman, however much I might wish to be.

And so I thanked him for his clemency, went up, and sat under the stars, which are said to be baleful on occasion. But the stars never did me harm, but were, in the bleak nights of captivity, a delight. I had often wished myself on one of them, for they are nearer to heaven than this earth, whose miseries God does not see and whose cries He no longer hears. I once believed that He hated His black creatures like a thing that's spoiled. I pictured Him as a crotchety old *massa* wearing a white suit and a Panama hat, who liked to sit on His porch of an evening and watch the sun setting on His property, drinking mint julips, and listening to the sad songs of His darkies.

When Israel was in Egypt's land:
Let my people go,
Oppress'd so hard they could not stand,
Let my People go.
Go down, Moses,
Way down in Egypt's land,
Tell old Pharaoh,
Let my people go.

I would have cursed God if I had not feared His scourge. I tasted cinders in my mouth. I tasted the salt of blood and the bitter herbs of humiliation.

With no one to pray to, I lay in the stern with my head on my arm, gnawing the rag-and-bone of my heart, until the threshing of the stern paddle put me to sleep. In the morning, I awoke, to find some canvas sacking thrown over me. I never knew who had done me this kindness. At the wharf, as I walked down the gangway, above nests of reeds and trash floating on the dark, oily water, the man who had choked me hissed, "Go back where you came from, nigger!" But by the action of some gracious, little-understood power, I was able to set the memory of a countervailing goodness against his enmity.

Stepping onto the pier, my legs buckled and I was sick—not in fear, but in reaction to the abruptly unmoving earth. A gull laughed in derision. I walked from Long Wharf the half mile to the *Christian Freeman* office, just along the street from here.

I was met by a farmer whose wife belonged to the Concord Female Anti-Slavery Society. He had been to Quincy Market, and the back of his wagon was littered with white beans, squash, and turnip greens. I relished the lingering odor of soil like a pleasure fondly remembered. I got up onto the seat next to him, and we traveled the twenty miles to Concord, where I first met Mr. Emerson. My clothes reeked of the *Grace's* coal smoke, a reminder that the stink of the inferno is strong enough to pollute even Paradise.

The farmer was silent during our drive and made no attempt to be untrue to his dour nature. I took his taciturnity as you would a courtesy: I preferred to be treated neither worse nor better than any other man. I would have been embarrassed by the strain of conversation, which did not come naturally to him. He did offer me chewing tobacco, which I could decline without fear of giving him offense.

And that, I thought, was proof of my emancipation. I might not have been a free man entirely in law—in slave states, I was neither free nor even a man—but on the seat of the lumbering wagon, I felt myself disenthralled by the ordinary business of men, freely transacted.

By sunset, I was standing in Concord's Monument Square, with the few articles of clothing I possessed in a satchel given me by the Quaker lady in Brooklyn. I felt like Lear without a kingdom, hearth, or even a heath to call his own. Like him, I would be obliged to live on the sufferance of others. As I write that line, I realize how ridiculous a simile it is, how self-aggrandizing. But let it stand. This slave's narrative is a record of his thoughts and feelings. No matter how wrongheaded or foolish they might appear, they are mine.

Mr. Bronson Alcott, an abolitionist and a station master of the Underground Railroad, arrived on foot, and together we walked to Emerson's house, called "Bush," on the Cambridge Turnpike.

My throat was parched, and I asked for water, which the young amanuensis brought me.

"How did you make your way during the first days of your exile?" asked Garrison, who appeared to have been spellbound by my recitation, unless I had been deceived by an effect of light playing on his spectacles' lenses that caused his eyes to shine.

"It was not exile," I said, undismayed by having contradicted him.

"No," he replied. "Jeroboam's plantation was no Eden from which to be cast out."

"Mr. Emerson had secured for me a place to live and also the means by which I could subsist. I worked for him and his Concord Transcendentalist friends, preparing and tending their vegetable gardens and orchards, doing what handiwork I could on their houses and outbuildings. I also worked every morning at the Mill-dam sawmill, sharpening blades and sweeping up the shavings. In my single-handed fashion, I made my way until I went to Walden Woods in order to be useful to Henry. I continue odd-jobbing, but I give him as much of my attention as he can tolerate."

"The motions of destiny are indeed bewildering," said Garrison.

The man whose arms were encased in sleeve-protectors made a guttural noise of assent.

Having concluded my autobiography, I shut my eyes as though to rid them of the vivid, often painful scenes that had passed before them. I had not told Garrison everything concerning my life as slave and fugitive. Whose memories are so comprehensive, whose powers of self-discovery so strong and honest that they can tell all? From my days and nights, I had selected some, which might or might not have been the most significant, according to the machinery of recollection, which I do not understand. Garrison, however, was delighted by my narrative and paid me the compliment of saying that mine was "as fine an accounting as that by Frederick Douglass." I was pleased that he had not shown astonishment at my fluency—that I was not, in his estimation, a "well-spoken negro."

"Mr. Douglass happens to be in Boston," said Garrison. "I am sure you two would have much to say to each other."

I lacked the audacity to meet a celebrated figure like Frederick Douglass. I had "crept up gradually" on Henry and on Emerson, as Sam Staples, the sheriff, had once said of me. I had grown accustomed to them as people and never gave much thought to their fame. But I could no more imagine meeting Mr. Douglass than I could the prophet Moses. Garrison, who was alert to others' feelings, must have sensed my confusion, because he said, "Another time, perhaps."

"Yes," I said. "Another time. I must be getting back to Concord. Mr. Hawthorne and I are going back together."

Four years ago, I did meet Mr. Douglass, in Washington City. We spent an agreeable hour in the lobby of the Willard Hotel, talking about the Mountain Meadows Massacre and the Utah War; the panic on Wall Street; Samuel Cartwright's book *Diseases and Peculiarities of the Negro Race*, proving that slaves who run away from their masters are stricken with a form of insanity called Drapetomania; President Buchanan's dictum "I acknowledge no master but the law"; and the Dred Scott decision, by which the Supreme Court confirmed the negroes' legal status as property. Neither of us was inclined to reminisce about his past life. It was better that way. Besides, what could one of us have said to the other to change or enlighten him? We were two fingers of the same hand; what one knew, the other did also by virtue of common blood and experience.

He did say this, as I recall: "Abolition will not put an end to slavery."

I thought at the time that he was wrong.

AT FIVE O'CLOCK, I WAS INSIDE the Lamb Tavern, waiting for Hawthorne to arrive. The elation I had felt when I left Garrison's office had faded into gloom. I had been in an expansive mood, but while I walked through the Boston streets to the tavern, I realized that the strength that had made me take heart was illusory. Neither unassailable freedom nor unfettered manhood was within my gift. I was beholden to Garrison, Emerson, Thoreau, Hawthorne—my life depended on their goodwill and the tolerance of others. I had no place that could not be taken from me, no possessions that could not be distrained. I could hold my head up just so high before risking the ax or the noose. A man hunter could break down the door to my cabin and, with no more than a warrant, drag me back to Virginia in chains.

Hawthorne arrived and sat at the table. His disheveled hair and clothing told of a man who had been anxious not to keep another man waiting, and for this civility, I was grateful.

"You've been in a great hurry, Nathaniel," I said, smiling.

"I have indeed," he said, mopping his overheated face with his handkerchief. "Pardon my lack of promptness."

"I've only just arrived myself," I said, determined not to brood.

We ordered ale. Hawthorne drank his in a single draft.

"What a thirst I had!"

"Did your business go well?" I asked, fascinated by a wisp of foam seeping into his dark mustache. I'm reminded of furbelows, I said to myself, recalling the drummer who had stood at the steamer rail, like an explorer taking possession of an undiscovered land in the name of an imperial majesty. Odd, how thoughts jump around in the mind like light reflected in a room from a moving cheval glass.

"Tolerably. And yours?"

"I believe so," I said noncommittally.

I was too exhausted to go into the matter. We were soon served our supper—game hens for Hawthorne, mackerel for me. Although I do not care for oily fish, I did not want to ape his choice. It was an insignificant gesture of independence, but I had no opportunity to make a larger one. Besides, I had not traveled to Boston for the purpose of dinner.

"I lost all track of time," he said, carving a pair of small birds on his plate. "At Alcott's suggestion, I visited the Chinese Museum, in the Marlboro Chapel on Washington Street. I saw many wonderful things—works of Oriental art, musical instruments, clothing, even a food called 'vermicelli.' But I was most intrigued by some remarkable toys made in Nanking. When wound with a key, they moved on their own. There was even a locomotive. What would little Eddy have said to that? They were not for sale—not that I have money for toys. As I walked here, I kept thinking about the Hebrew story of the golem. Do you know it, Samuel?"

"A creature made of mud that was brought to life by the breath of God. Like Adam."

"Stranger than he, I think. It is said that a rabbi succeeded in creating a golem, which saved the city of Prague from destruction. The creature had no will of its own and was compelled to do as the rabbi ordered."

I recalled how a Haitian slave woman would make moppets of straw and rough effigies of clay. She prayed to Ogún that the master or mistress, driver or breaker would be laid waste. None was that I knew of.

"I would like to write such a tale," he said, picking at the delicate bones. "How a man or woman can be helpless against something adventitious—or, better yet, how we can be at the mercy of impulses originating too deep within ourselves for recognition. Perhaps we are wound up by a key. . . ."

I had had too much experience of that key to comment. For me, it was real and not an idle fancy on which to build a tale. I could almost feel it in my back; the scars it had left were still there. I leaned against the hard chair and winced in order to remind myself of their reality. I was often impatient with authors, for whom life was a tangle of thoughts to untangle. Garrison knows how a rope feels around the neck and that a man is seldom delivered from the mortal complication of a lynch mob's noose.

Hawthorne had gone on to talk about Emerson.

"I spoke harshly of our friend and your 'benefactor' this morning, although you might not care for the word. It *is* patronizing. But there is nothing patronizing about Mr. Emerson. No, I wronged him when I said he was indifferent to the exigencies of ordinary life and people. His purposes are loftier than mine. I mean only to be successful and get Sophia and me out of debt. Ours is a genteel poverty, I hasten to add. I would appear ridiculous in the eyes of someone who has known privation such as yours, Samuel, to talk of hardship."

I made a noise at the back of my throat, signifying tolerance.

"To be truthful, which I try to be, I'm uncomfortable sitting here with you—not for the reason you may suppose: I have no prejudice. I consider you an intelligent and amiable fellow, companionable in my own habitual silences. But you are a constant reminder—a rebuke—to my race, Samuel, and I cannot help feeling guilty in your presence."

I knew all there was to know about guilt.

"It's damn awkward! I don't know whether to ignore the fact that you are a black man or insist on it. Whatever I do is likely to cause offense, which I do not intend or want. How are the two races to come together at last if we find it difficult to spend an hour over dinner?"

"I don't find it so," I said, lying.

"Then you are a better man than I am. Let me change the subject."

He changed it to Henry.

"He is the most unmalleable fellow alive—the most tedious, irksome, and intolerable—the narrowest and most notional—and yet, true as all this is, he has qualities of intellect and character I cannot help but envy."

He went on to assay Henry's character: his industry and indolence . . . sociability and misanthropy . . . courtesy and incivility . . . openhandedness and meanness . . . originality and—

With a distracted air, he finished his meal, wiped his greasy lips, and continued his analysis as if he had been a phrenologist and had Henry's skull before him to read with his fingertips.

"He is a magpie of other people's ideas, Waldo's in particular. He relies too much on figurative language at the expense of an accurate notation of the natural world, whose essentials he claims to understand. He's an idler and a shirker. For all that, Samuel, I respect him. His friendship means a good deal to me."

After a while, I didn't know if Hawthorne was talking about two different men or about one man—Henry—who, like one of Walden Pond's eels, was too slippery to grasp. I kept my eyes fixed on Hawthorne's but let my mind wander, while he expatiated at a length that would have astonished anyone who knew him. I heard someone make a joke, someone laugh, someone begin a song and end it abruptly, someone curse under his breath, a chair scraped back in anger, someone cough, and the flu rattle in the chimney to let out the smoke that had suddenly bloomed inside the sooty tavern walls.

"I've never asked what *you* think of Henry," said Hawthorne, having reached the end of his appraisal. "Or perhaps you think it indiscreet to talk about him. . . ."

"Not at all," I said, trying to sound like a man of the world. "I also admire him."

I did admire Henry, although I heard a faint antiphon of mistrust inside my head. My appreciation of his qualities would increase when he began to walk the woods with a notched stick and paddle the ponds with a plumb line to sound their depths. With those rude instruments, he took the rough measure of the world beyond his fancy. He became less like Emerson and more like Hawthorne, less an idealist and more a pragmatist. Since then, however, I have come to believe that the largest truths often lie in the figures we make of them.

"The world admires Henry, except for a peevish few in Concord and its environs who call him harebrained, a crackpot, and a 'woods burner,'" said Hawthorne.

He was alluding to an accident two years before, when Henry fell asleep by Fairhaven Bay and, having left his fire unattended, it burned down three hundred acres of woodland. Had the wind been in the right quarter, the fire would have scorched the town. Some never forgave him for the destruction of their woodlots, and Henry never did make good their losses.

"Should a man's foibles be taxed when preparing a final statement of his worth?" asked Hawthorne. "Or should they be brushed aside like the shavings of a pencil sharpened without a thought to tidiness and used to set down on paper a truth of the mind or eye?"

Having no answer to make, I said, "He spends much of his time at his writing desk."

"Sentences don't make themselves as oysters do pearls," said Hawthorne. "And will you write your story?"

I guessed then that Emerson had spoken of my odious

conduct at Freemasons' Hall, and I damned him silently for not having kept it from Hawthorne. I was embarrassed and weary of a conversation that had prolonged itself beyond supper and on to whiskey and cigars, purchased by me for both of us with the money remaining from Emerson's largesse in order to spite him.

"I cannot write," I said irritably.

My mouth burned with drink, my nostrils with smoke.

"Doubtless, Henry Bibb, Moses Roper, Solomon Northup, and Frederick Douglass thought as much—or as little of themselves. Henry likes to say that 'ancient trees can put forth rare blossoms.' Likewise, misery can sharpen a dull nib and transmute iron gall to ink."

Much later, I would read the slave narrative of Henry Bibb. In it, he wrote:

> I was brought up in the Counties of Shelby, Henry, Oldham, and Trimble. Or, more correctly speaking, in the above counties, I may safely say, I was *flogged up*; for where I should have received moral, mental, and religious instruction, I received stripes without number, the object of which was to degrade and keep me in subordination. I can truly say, that I drank deeply of the bitter cup of suffering and woe.

Bibb had made that cup his ink pot, and the bitter drink had instilled in him eloquence, which was that of a man who sought to tell the truth about himself by every means of which utterance is capable. The truth lies beyond our eyes' power to perceive. The obscurity that defied Henry's measuring stick, cod line and stone plumb, and spyglass was pierced by his symbols. Literature is the "city upon a hill," for which John Winthrop yearned; it is the Celestial City atop Mount Zion, which John Bunyan sought; it is the place where meaning waits to be discovered. All this I know now to be the case.

"I saw poor Bill Wheeler shambling down Monument Street on the stumps of his legs, long after the parading militia had passed him, as though he was determined to catch up with it," said Hawthorne, peering into his empty glass as if expecting to find meaning there. "I felt sorry for him; his solitary life must be a trial. Henry wondered if he might not be better off as he was; that, in his estrangement, he might enjoy a secret communion with nature. I remember having given him a sharp look, which he appeared not to notice."

I thought Hawthorne's observations on the contradictory nature of humankind naïve.

Having finished our supper and settled with the landlord, we walked across the Common to our hotel. We paused to watch a dark solitary shape walk beneath a lamppost and, having left its ring of light, disappear. I was prepared to hear him comment on the fugitive quality of life, but Hawthorne had nothing to say on this or any other subject. His unusual volubility had spent itself at supper. I was glad of the silence, which I, too, considered companionable. I looked up and found the Drinking Gourd, called by some the Big Dipper and by others the Great Bear. Following the two stars of its cup with my eyes, I found the North Star, which has shown the way to freedom for so many of my people.

> When the sun comes back
> And the first quail calls,
> Follow the Drinking Gourd.
> For the old man is waiting
> For to carry you to freedom,
> If you follow the Drinking Gourd.

With a suddenness that could have made me cry out had I not been used to keeping my feelings in check, I realized that the star that had been, for us, like the one that had shed its light on the place where Jesus lay in a manger did not shine on America. The shepherds and the magi had followed theirs to a stable in Bethlehem, but ours did not point to Boston or Maine or to any other part of the Union. *Our* Bethlehem lay farther north, in Canada, where slavers' laws did not apply and man hunters came as thieves and outlaws liable to arrest. I shuddered to think how precariously I occupied the little space I called mine, in Concord. My safety was illusory, my status as doubtful as it had been in Virginia—no, it was more so: On the plantation, in slave shacks and in the mistress's kitchen, I had known my place.

"It's a lovely night," said Hawthorne.

"Yes."

"We'll make an early start tomorrow. The packet boat to Salem leaves at six; your train, at quarter past seven. I'll be in Concord again in a week or two."

We went inside the hotel and parted with a handshake at the foot of the staircase; Hawthorne had a room on the second floor; mine was in the attic. I lay in bed under the rafters of the pitched roof like an overturned boat, waiting for sleep to take me. I thought over the crowded day's events. While I had traveled little in Boston, in my mind and nerves, I had relived a long journey spent in misery and fear, and I was exhausted.

IV

aving returned to Concord, I went immediately to Bush. I felt I owed Emerson an accounting of my meeting with Garrison. I would neglect to tell him that I had squandered his money on whiskey and cigars. While I waited in his study, I could not help but think of him as a being—a golem, if you like—endued with the musty breath of foxed paper and the ancient dust of libraries. But I may have been wrong. It is easy to misjudge others—a commonplace remark, but nonetheless true. We close our minds to the completeness of others, striking from the portraits we draw of them in our imaginations all contradiction. Emerson was not afraid to contradict himself, which gave him license to contradict others. His criticism was never harsh, unlike, say, that of Edgar Poe, whose barbs could wound.

"Good afternoon, Samuel," said Emerson cheerfully, coming into the study. "I've been weeding the garden. Henry is not the only one who enjoys a bit of dirt on his hands."

Emerson could make prosaic matters sound like parables.

"Good afternoon, Mr. Emerson. I hope you've been well."

"Well enough. It's Lidian who worries me, as always," he said as he sat behind his desk.

"Is she poorly?" I asked sincerely, for I liked the lady and knew her to be often ill.

"The old complaint. She is resting in her room." When I shut my eyes, I could see her pinched face in the shadow of her mobcap. "Your visit to Boston with Mr. Hawthorne—it went well?"

I told him about my visit. Of my narrative, I said only that it would be published in *The Liberator.*

"I'm glad of it. That much lies within your people's power to effect change."

His head swiveled like an owl's from the contemplation of his long, slender fingers, raised into a steeple, to regard my face.

"Don't be offended, Samuel. You are a man—I would not have you think that I consider you otherwise. But laws bent to evil purposes have in some ways unmanned you. Your people are powerless because they are so in law. By my saying 'your people,' I am making a racial distinction, which, regardless of my intention, contributes to the division between us. All that you can do is to testify, as earnestly as is in your power, against injustice. You must do the little that has been left for you to do, and that little is the publication of your narrative."

I had been somewhat distracted by a fly at the windowpane, noisy in its disgruntlement to be let out. But I had heard enough of what Emerson had to say concerning my duty to my race. I would have been satisfied to bring hell fire down on Jeroboam's head, never mind his damned frock-coated fraternity. If I prayed for anything, it was for the pleasure of seeing him torn limb from limb, his bowels pulled out, roasted, and fed to his pigs.

"What's to be done with me, Mr. Emerson?" I asked after his voice had died in the room, to be reborn one day in the ears of posterity.

"Done with you?"

"Am I always to live like this?" My empty sleeve took in Emerson's study, as if the answer to my question lay there.

All at once, I was determined to reveal myself to him as I was, a man uncertain of his place and future, unafraid to show a white man his discontent. He sat back in his chair and regarded me solemnly. I think I must have held my breath.

"You have aspirations," said Emerson, his voice modulating into thoughtfulness.

He must have believed that I was satisfied to live as a virtually free man in Concord, within earshot of the Lyceum and the "academy" over which he tranquilly presided—a Socrates who would never be offered the fatal hemlock.

"Yes," I replied in a tone that I hoped sounded dignified.

"That's as it should be," he said. "I have been insensitive. What would you like to do, Samuel?"

I had no idea, not having pondered an answer to a question I believed would never be asked of me. I replied impulsively, "A teacher." I was acquainted with Emerson well enough to know that only lofty ambitions could please him. I don't believe I was frivolous in wanting to be well dressed someday besides being well-spoken.

He was radiant.

"As a colored teacher of colored children, you can be of

inestimable value to your race." We both knew that there would be no opportunity to teach white children. "I have friends on the faculty of Middlebury College, in Vermont. The college admits negroes. I'll write to find out what can be done for you."

"Thank you, Mr. Emerson. I'm grateful."

I put out my hand, and he took it.

He was as good as his word: I matriculated in the fall of 1848 at Middlebury. The year before that, he had gotten up a subscription to pay for my freedom. Ellery Channing, Bronson Alcott and his daughter Louisa May, Henry's father, John Thoreau, Elizabeth Peabody, Margaret Fuller, the Wards—even, it has been my constant pleasure to recall, Charles Dickens, Thomas Carlyle, Longfellow, James Russell Lowell, and Sam Staples, who had reluctantly jailed Henry for refusing to pay his poll tax—all contributed.

"You have a gift," said Emerson. I had none that I could see. "A natural felicity."

"I read the Bible and *The Pilgrim's Progress*," I said to impress him.

"I admire what you've managed to accomplish, Samuel. You should do well at Middlebury." He took a bound copy of his essay "Self-Reliance" from a desk drawer and inscribed it to me with his best wishes. I accepted the gift with a show of gratitude.

I left Bush in an exultant mood. Nothing had been settled: The college was unaware of my existence, as defined by the laws that sought to confirm or deny it, and the idea of my legal emancipation from Jeroboam had yet to be entertained, proposed, and executed. As far as my master knew, I was a fugitive, with no more claim to liberty than a parlor chair that had decided to walk off in search of a promised land for furniture. Nonetheless, I sensed a change in the air, as if the wind had swung on its hinge away from the noxious Slough of Despond, in which I had been mired, to the Delectable Mountains, where all sweet things await us. *Selah*!

Outside in the dooryard, I took off my coat and chopped wood to last several days. I did so because I wanted to. Emerson stood at the window, but I could not see his face clearly behind the imperfect glass.

"The imperfections are there so that we should be reminded of the glass and our presence on the wrong side of it," I once overheard Henry tell Lidian, who had been industriously rubbing a window clean of smudges.

"Nonsense, Mr. Thoreau!" she cried with a laugh. "You see symbols where none exists."

I WAS SCOURING MY CABIN FLOOR with sand when Henry knocked. I unlocked the door and invited him inside.

"There's no point in locking it," he said, wiping his boot soles on the grass outside.

"What brings you here?" I asked, to change the subject, one which was of long standing between us.

"I've come to ask you to a picnic by Fairhaven Bay." He had taken off his hat and was holding it like a collection plate. "Hawthorne's in town for a meeting of the Transcendental Club. I've borrowed Hosmer's boat."

"When?" I asked. I had no plans, but I wished to appear like someone who did.

"Tomorrow, at nine o'clock. We'll meet at Egg Rock and travel up the Sudbury to the bay."

I knew that stretch of river, having often walked it with Henry. There were excellent huckleberries and sweet black-berries to be had there, if one did not mind being nettled. I had grown up (or been "flogged up," in Henry Bibb's color-ful variant) in nature, as though I had been an aborigine—rain, dirt, mud, and cold had been my elements. But I had looked upon the outdoors as a space in which to toil. That it could also be a place in which to play was an alien notion.

"I'd like to go," I said.

"Good."

He was in one of his laconic moods, and I thought he would leave me to get on with my floor. Instead, he sat in the "visitor's chair" and watched me scrub.

"Nothing like Walden sand for purity, or its ice, either."

I knew he was thinking about the Carlson boy. His memory would cast a shadow over Henry's sunny nature. During the winter, when he had resolved to measure the depths of the pond, we drilled holes all across the ice and then dropped a plumb line to the bottom. When icy water spurted through the hole, Henry shrank back like a man afraid to step in something disagreeable.

I did not care to dwell on death, having been overly acquainted with it. I concentrated my attention on the floorboards, which had become smooth and glossy under my ministrations.

"How does your journal grow?" I asked, thinking of the nursery rhyme that I had been humming all morning.

"Like snow on a window ledge," he replied. "The more it piles up, the less I can see of what's outside."

"You're too hard on yourself, Henry."

"Maybe."

He chewed thoughtfully on a stem of tasseled grass.

"Why do you let the devil ride you?" I scolded him, knowing he was too lost in thought to care—or to get up on his high horse, the way he sometimes did.

"He does have his spurs in me!" Self-mockery made him likable.

"Nobody will mind if you stop," I said to be spiteful.

"You're right, Samuel."

"I don't see that it gives you pleasure to be shut up so much indoors."

"If I could only go about with a telegraph key in my pocket!"

More whimsies!

"What's this, some sort of talisman?"

He had picked up a small tribal god from my windowsill. I had carved it out of pitch pine. I liked the smell of it.

"Something I whittled."

"It has a strong face. Your gods are crude, but powerful."

"They're not my gods," I said, annoyed. "I'm a Methodist when I'm anything at all."

"Don't let Waldo hear you say that. Just the thought of Methodists gives him boils."

Henry was weighing the carved wood in his hand like

someone attempting to discover the worth of a thing with no use that he could see.

"Take it," I said on impulse.

I was kneeling, as if in terror or humility, but I was only scrubbing a floor.

"How's that?" he asked, cupping an ear.

"I want you to have it."

How I relished the thought of making him a gift!

"Well, thank you, Samuel. It's most kind of you. I'll put it on my writing desk, next to the pinecone from the White Mountains and the water-moccasin skin John found on the bank of the Merrimack. It may inspire a journal entry."

With my knife, I had reached deeply into Henry—into his vitals—and carved a symbol more ancient than the cross there. I pictured my rude figurine taking its luminous place in the firmament of his mind. Was he thinking of my carving when, later, he wrote in *Walden*, "One hastens to southern Africa to chase the giraffe; but surely that is not the game he would be after. How long, pray, would a man hunt giraffes if he could? Snipes and woodcocks also may afford rare sport; but I trust it would be nobler game to shoot one's self"?

He sat awhile longer in my hut, holding the effigy on his palm, spellbound—listening, it seemed to me, to a distant voice that may or may not have been an African one while I swept the floor clean of sand. I can often be persuaded of the most nonsensical ideas. His face appeared not homely, as Hawthorne had described it, but tragic. Beneath the sunburned flesh, I thought I saw the ivory of his skull as it would come to be in time. I sensed his weariness, which might have been the consumption that one day would finish him. Perhaps he was tired of being in eternal opposition to society, to decorum, to law, to the Almighty—to all that is not natural, which is the greater portion of man's world. While he sat in the waning light, was he listening to harmonies beyond my hearing? There were moments during the year I spent in his company—under his spell, fight it as I may!—that I loved him, however grudgingly. As the withdrawing light shadowed his face, I sensed something else about Henry Thoreau: a thwarted desire for intimacy, an incapacity common to us both.

"Henry . . ."

I judged that the moment had arrived when our acquaintance could be promoted to something more closely resembling friendship.

"What is it, Samuel?"

Just then, a squirrel came through the doorway with quick little jumps. It raced into a corner of the hut, raising a chitter of protest and alarm.

"It is not a symbol, Henry," Henry said, admonishing himself with a smile that included me. "It is only a squirrel."

I chased it back outside with a broom.

We embarked at Egg Rock, at a little after nine o'clock. Hawthorne worked the tiller; Henry and I rowed. Useless in the nearly breathless morning air, the sail was reefed. In spite of my handicap, we rowed well together, and the boat made headway against a gentle current. The midges rose and reassembled on the water with each stroke of the oars, whose blades from time to time were lifted out of the river, draped in green and brown weeds.

Henry reminisced about his and John's trip down the Concord River to the Merrimack. I listened with half an ear, wishing I might remove my shirt like Henry, now that the sweat had begun to dampen it, but I was shy of letting them see a back italicized by the whip. I did not want the issue of slavery and abolition raised, as it surely would have been. I wanted to enjoy an ordinary day on the river, like a man unconstrained by bad luck or a spiteful destiny.

"I overheard Sam Staples reading from the Boston paper how the Knickerbockers fell to the Brooklyn Club last week in Hoboken, twenty-three to one," I said, to put the conversation on a mundane course. In truth, I cared nothing for boyish pastimes.

"I used to enjoy the cricket matches when I lived in Boston," said Hawthorne, lolling in the stern. The mildness of the current and his two oarsmen's steadiness made his effort at the tiller almost negligible. I could see that Henry was becoming vexed by his friend's nonchalance and that no small talk was going to please him. So long as the talk did not concern me, they could bicker all they wanted.

"I suggest we take turns," said Henry at last, shipping his oar. Before I could ship mine, the boat had traced a semi-circle on the water like a Jesus bug.

"Certainly," said Hawthorne, straightening our course. "I always meant to do my fair share of work. I was a communalist, remember."

He let go of the tiller and began to make his way forward before we had agreed which of us—Henry or me—would relieve him. There followed a comical scene in which we three jostled and the boat rocked crazily, so that I feared we would soon fall overboard. Henry stood, obliging Hawthorne to take a step backward. Then I stood and clambered into the bow, leaving the seat empty. Henry and Hawthorne danced clumsily—the boat yawing—until they had exchanged places, leaving Henry free to take the tiller and Hawthorne to pick up an oar. I returned to mine, and together we dug our blades into the river, and the boat lurched toward our destination, which lay, according to Henry, now less than two miles to the south.

Henry began to sing the ditty that he and John had sung, buoyantly, during their boat trip into New Hampshire: "Row, brothers, row, the stream runs fast." Hawthorne and I hummed in concert, and any chance spark of controversy, resulting from the division of labor and our clog dance aboard the boat, appeared to have been dampened.

Motioning toward the alder trees mirrored on the river's untroubled surface, Hawthorne remarked, "I am half convinced that the reflection is indeed the reality."

Henry replied, "I used to think the same, but lately I've been coming round to the idea that reality can be grasped by patient, careful observation. You can't build a railroad across a surface of reflections, no matter how picturesque. It requires bedrock, timber, and iron."

As if to illustrate his point, a muskrat slunk through the reeds, then jumped into the river, shattering the liquid mirror and the trees' reflections it had held.

"I thought you disapproved of railroads."

"I do. But as a symbol, they are useful. I'm afraid,

Nathaniel, that the railroads are here to stay. Once conceived, an idea—good or bad—cannot be canceled or annulled. They'll lay a track across hell, if the vested interests have their way."

I rode on it, I said to myself. From Virginia to Concord—no return ticket, if you please.

"Symbols again! Didn't you just tell me you'd forsworn them?"

"I said no such thing! Besides, I forswear nothing except narrow-mindedness."

Hawthorne grunted.

"Would you like to trade places again, Nathaniel?"

What about me? I wondered in annoyance.

"You remind me of a galley slave during the Punic Wars," Henry said to his friend. And then he recited a few lines in Latin.

At the word *slave,* Hawthorne had turned a little on his seat to regard my face, which I kept expressionless.

I have often wondered whether the laws governing dreams and those governing thought are identical: One thing leads to another and thence to some other, by a concatenation of ideas, figments, and vagaries bound by a secret logic, which, on the face of it, seems absurd.

Henry pinched his nostrils, the left, then the right, and blew to rid them of snot. By such homely details, not found in their biographies, do eminent men come to life for us. Hawthorne betrayed his disgust by looking at his well-tended hands. I wondered what Emerson would have said about his protégé's uncouthness. Emerson was as polished as a chestnut, while Henry was rough as bark.

Emerson could look dignified sitting on a tuffet, while Henry would not have looked so on a throne. He was a mixture of self-knowledge and unself-consciousness. I never did assay what proportion one occupied in relation to the other. I would have to leave it to the higher mathematics of the world to come.

I was spent in this one; I could not have pulled my oar again to save my life. I let it fall idle in the water. I gazed at the cardinal flowers spotting the riverbank's meadows. I wished I might rest among them or walk farther off into the sandy uplands, among the trees whose green masses I could see swelling with a wind unavailable to us on the river.

"I'm all done in," I said.

Both men were embarrassed because they had been insensitive to the hardship of rowing upriver, even in relatively slack water, for a one-handed man. I had held my own almost beyond the limits of my endurance to prove to them and to myself that I was their equal at least in *this*. I had exhausted my reserves, however, and no longer cared what they thought of me.

Henry relieved me at the oar, and I took the tiller.

"We're yours to command," said Hawthorne, saluting me with only a hint of irony.

"Take up your oars, gentlemen, and row," I said graciously.

The boat jumped forward when the oars bit into the river. I listened to them creak in the oarlocks and to the planked hull grumble. Manual labor makes a pretty music to the ear of idle men. Even a chain will ring out merrily for those who own and drive and break others. For the moment, we were in the river's keeping, although it had long ago forgotten the way to Fairhaven Bay, except as blood knows the route through the body's sluices and thoughts through the brain's gray tangle. The boat moved by small jerks, interrupting a glassy suspense in which Henry and Hawthorne again considered the great themes of nature.

"The natural man is an unfinished one," said Hawthorne.

"Would you send the Indians to finishing school?" jeered Henry.

"They are imprudent," replied Hawthorne, unruffled. "They trust too much in whatever providential hand they acknowledge."

Like most of us, I thought.

Henry retorted, "They spend no more than they need and take only as much as can be replenished and restored. They are earth's true husbandmen."

Only men with the means to be idle could have such an argument as this, I thought.

Hawthorne countered, saying, "*You* are not the natural man that you suppose." Henry bristled, and the flat of his oar spanked the water's surface. "You're too well armed with Greek and Latin references, with saws and maxims, with your opinions and conceits. Do you suppose that the Penobscot Indians keep accounts?"

"Yes, but not as Shattuck the grocer does, or even as I do."

"My point," said Hawthorne. "Grocers see the world though ledger sheets, poets through staves and stanzas."

"Alas, not being of savage birth, I must read nature at second hand," said Thoreau with a sulk.

Civilized men have lost the key to Eden's gate, I thought, and will never find it again.

"You are not usually so argumentative, Nathaniel."

"Sometimes I like to provoke you."

"I am not provoked!" said Henry, his voice strained by irritation.

His oar missed a beat, and the boat slewed. At the time, I believed that Henry was too conscious of nature to be entirely at home in it. One needed to be like the squirrel, lacking judgment and a mind able to ponder nature's meaning and purposes. The squirrel gives no thought to its future, beyond burying acorns against winter's famine. Filling journals with thoughts on the natural world, as Henry did compulsively, was like stuffing pillows with feathers, an occupation that reveals little about chickens. Like a boy who sees in his father's calloused hands only dirt under the nails, I was determined to misunderstand Henry Thoreau and his experiment in simplicity.

"The ancients made much of rivers," said Henry, like a man casting about for a change of subject. "They are the great figure for time, of course."

Hawthorne grimaced in exertion or at the obviousness of the remark. Henry took it as an insult to his originality, which he wore like an eccentric's hat. At that time, I found it hard to tell a sincere man from a poseur. In these pages, reader, Henry is not necessarily as he was, but as he seemed to me.

"I assure you, Nathaniel, that I will not make the same mistake as the fly."

"Which is?"

"To annoy the ear with meaningless buzzing."

"All is *buzz, buzz, buzz*," said Hawthorne with uncustomary petulance.

Having felt an insect settle on my cheek, I swatted it. My palm made a resounding slap. Hawthorne laughed, and Henry frowned, thinking I had meant to mock him.

"I had something other than platitudes in mind," he said with a sniff, as if an unpleasant odor had invaded his nostrils. "I meant to say that we carry our own time with us to the end, just as this boat is carrying us on a river indifferent to our petty aims and histories and obedient only to the great sweep of time until we are crushed on the rocks waiting to receive us."

I thought then that Henry was right, and nothing in the intervening years has changed my mind.

"Still, I would not exchange my time—the one that beats for me—for a past or a future that seems more glamorous or novel, no more than I would change my shirt because it has gone out of fashion, but only if, having become out at the elbows, it no longer serves its purpose. 'Thy gowns, thy shoes, thy beds of roses, / Thy cap, thy kirtle, and thy posies / Soon break, soon wither, soon forgotten, / In folly ripe, in reason rotten.' Sir Walter."

Great men will often speak as if for the ages, though their audience be only a black man in a boat going nowhere except a bay that might just as well have been called a pond, for it was not much larger than Walden.

The keel scythed through a stand of water lilies. The startled frogs jumped from their green pads, turtles pulled in their heads, and a sunfish sought its own eclipse in the perpetual darkness of the riverbed.

The two Olympians considered next the lilies of the field, a sentimental economy close to Henry's irreligious heart. But I will spare you their tiresome "shuttlecock."

When we arrived at Fairhaven Bay, the ice that Hawthorne had brought with him to keep our boiled eggs fresh had melted in the summer heat, regardless of its insulating thatch of hay.

I am thinking at this moment of poor John Franklin and his men, famished aboard the icebound *Erebus* and *Terror*, near King William Island, in the Arctic's Victoria Strait. While we were having our river outing—pleasant despite the spoiled eggs—they had been dead some weeks or months. What had *they* made of nature? I cannot help thinking of my "heroic voyage" down Ballard Creek to Ragged Island. No . . . To call it a voyage is to exalt what a log or a muskrat does mindlessly; to call it heroic is equally false, since I was in terror for my life and would have crawled through ooze and muck to escape the vengeful rod. Fear, not beauty or love or even ambition, is the great driver of men and women. What a book I could write! I thought then. This one, in fact. I had meant to take out a few of memory's things from my valise, so to speak, and find that I have been unpacking a portmanteau or a magician's tall hat, from which there seems to be no end of scarves and rabbits. Writing, too, is a river in whose irresistible current we embark, sail, and, with luck, disembark with our shoes and tobacco dry.

The meadow on either side of the Sudbury was flooded.

I might have steered a course through it as I had once seen Hawthorne do across the Old Manse's lawn after a heavy rain had brought the Concord River nearly to his doorstep. Watching him sail *Pond Lily* where cows had grazed was, I think, the most perfect image of freedom I have ever seen. What is freedom if not to go wherever the spirit wills, careless of restraints and accidental hindrances like the banks and beds of a river?

"I haven't been in Adam's Woods since I burned them down," said Thoreau.

In Adam's Woods . . .

"Damn 'woods burner!'" jibed Hawthorne, invoking Henry's misadventure with char cloth and a phosphorus match.

"It was a glorious spectacle!" said Henry, pleased with himself.

You will 'know' a woman but not love.

A light wind arose, agitating the river water into chop slapping at our bow. The moment was confused by the spice of wild primrose, the rattle and trill of a marsh wren, the reeling of the azure sky. The rudder shivered, and I felt a thrill in my hand; the tiller might have been endued with a mind all its own. I had not yet passed beyond the magnetism of my superstitious youth, with its stories of the strange practices of Haitian slaves, for whom a stick held aloft could, and did, conduct spirits from the next world into this. The yew-wood tiller throbbed with desire that might have belonged to the river, a naiad, or the ghost of the young woman Fenda Freeman had been long before she foresaw my coming to Adam's Woods. It prodded me to steer toward the meadow. The meadow might have wished it, and the boat also. I could not help thinking there might be a woman waiting for me on the far side of the marsh grass, where the sandy uplands rose. But I did not waver; I held fast while Henry and Hawthorne rowed against the current—its desires as heedless of my own as were theirs, and just as secret.

"*But not love!*" I had shouted the words to myself, but they had escaped my mouth, so fervent had been the thought behind the utterance.

"What's wrong, Samuel?" asked Hawthorne, who had been silent, as was his custom, while Henry had been chattering about river grapes.

"Nothing," I said. But then I was moved to speak my mind. "I feel knotted up."

"The strain on your arm," said Henry sympathetically.

"Will you please be quiet!" I cried with strength enough to make an egret shy from its solitary angling in the marsh grass. I did not want Henry's sympathy; I wanted his hatred to chew on like rancid meat.

"I don't understand you, Samuel!" he replied sharply.

"Must you always talk so?"

A passion had been kindled in me by an obscure emotion that belittled me. I knew it, but I fumed nonetheless.

"Talking is an art of civilized men," said Henry patiently, as if to a child.

"And of Margaret Fuller," said Hawthorne to his boot tops, where his eyes had lighted in embarrassment.

"I'm sick of art and sick of civilized men," I muttered.

I don't know what possessed me. I was like a clock that cannot fathom its own inner workings.

Henry took off his straw hat, and his face and eyes came out of their eclipse. I saw—or thought I did—a person clear and frank as the bottom of a lake when the sun is momentarily put out by a passing cloud. In his nut brown, weather-beaten face and weak chin, I saw Henry Thoreau for what he was: generous and mean, gregarious and reclusive, gentle and uncouth, erudite and common, confident and afraid, as are we all.

"I apologize," he said, without elaborating, and then he put on his hat again.

I nodded and let the tiller lie lightly in my hand.

At Fairhaven Bay, our boat came to rest on the graveled beach with a pleasing scrape of her hull against the pale yellow pebbles that ground underfoot when we walked up onto the shore. Henry had forgiven me my outburst; he was not one to hold a grudge or nurse a grievance. Hawthorne appeared to be embarrassed still as he busied himself with housekeeping. He shook out a tablecloth and laid it—a nicety Henry scorned—set out bread and smoked meat, while Henry cut melons he had grown and brought as his contribution to the feast. I took a cane pole from the boat and a worm from the tangled knot inside a tobacco tin and threaded it on a hook. Bream, pike, and hornpout were ample in the bay, and we had come prepared to make a supper of them on our return to Concord.

While I fished, the two men ate and talked. Henry was

more garrulous than his usually reticent friend. I listened to them with half an ear. I thought about the underside of things—fish always brought it to mind. Theirs is a dark and liquid world where all is vaguely seen and heard, remote from ours, though we have only to dangle a morsel of bread or meat to rip them out of their universe and into ours, where the rock is waiting to cudgel them, the knife to disembowel them, and the fire to cook what flesh remains, in a pan or on a stick held to the flames. Do fish fear them, the instruments of their destruction? Is their fate common knowledge with them—born or bred in their tiny brains or wherever fear, which is only the keenest of expectations, lies? Maybe there is an organ, the color of gall, where terror awaits the cruel ascent—or the Rapture, if fish have an instinct for resurrection into the waters of the firmament. Foreboding yields in an instant to the bitter recognition of hook, stone, knife, and fire comprising their sad destiny.

In slave pens and hovels where we laid our heads in silence, I would shrink into the darkness behind my closed eyes—there, to work out the reason for my having been born or, more often, to take refuge in a night given over to forgetfulness, where oleander and jasmine sweetened the foul air of our sty and rare words of kindness were sown like bread for careless birds. Prodded by whip handle, boot, or the light from a lantern rudely unshuttered with a rasp near my face, I would open my eyes in bitter recognition of my own sad destiny.

What, I wondered, could nature have meant by us?

"I have imagined a forest," said Hawthorne, gesturing toward Adam's Woods.

They had been talking about—what else?—nature. It was their common meat—more so for Henry; but Hawthorne, Emerson, Ellery Channing, Margaret Fuller—they all went at it like starvelings, ardently and avidly, with knife and fork, hammer and tongs. They would suck it to the marrow and then lick the greasy bones.

"A wilderness, dark, vast, and impenetrable stretching from the ancient world to the new. I could walk from Walden Woods to Germania's Schwarzwald or to the Charcoal Forest of the Franks—"

"An ocean and fifteen hundred years separate them," said Henry, snorting in derision.

"In my mind. I could walk there in my mind. Don't be contrarious!"

"Walden is enough for me."

"The woods I have in mind survive only as a fable for the darkness in which we are engulfed, never mind the light from our lamps and tapers, which are only a little less sooty and dangerous than savage torches."

"A greasy torch is the very thing with which to burn down our sacred institutions."

"Henry, you're a pyromaniac!" said Hawthorne with a smile before returning to his theme. "I've been thinking of the primeval forest as it might be a symbol for what overcasts the mind with gloom and shadows the human heart, like lake water stained by cedar trees. To have lived always in a penumbra—light strained by a roof thatched by thickset leaves and branches—must have contributed a somber portion to their souls and, as heirs to their melancholy, to our own."

For Transcendentalists, the soul is not an illumination kindled by stained glass and the glint of silver chalices, but the mind on fire, as if lighted to drive off wolves.

"Nathaniel, I'm not the least melancholy," said Henry, eating a piece of melon.

"I am," replied Hawthorne without affectation.

Of the two men, I loved Hawthorne more. Despite his attractive appearance, he stood uncomfortably apart from his fellows. A dark seam ran through his nature, and his gentle eyes were often sad.

"An inviolate forest undiminished by human law—an intimation of a higher truth!" he said with the fervor of a heretic, who did not quite believe in his heresy.

"A forest, being an aspect of nature, is itself a higher truth and not an intimation of one," said Henry, his beard glistening with melon juice.

Oh, he could be crotchety!

"While we were coming up the Sudbury, I composed a paragraph in my head," said Hawthorne, who then recited it from memory:

> "Letting the eyes follow along the course of the stream, they could catch the reflected light from its water, at some short distance within the forest, but soon lost all traces of it amid the bewilderment of tree-trunks and underbrush, and here and there a huge rock, covered over with gray lichens. All these giant trees and boulders of granite seemed

intent on making a mystery of the course of this small brook; fearing, perhaps, that, with its never-ceasing loquacity, it should whisper tales out of the heart of the old forest whence it flowed . . ."

"The Sudbury is more accurately described as a river and not a small brook," said Henry with deliberate pedantry in order to vex his friend.

"I wasn't describing the Sudbury or any other particular watercourse."

"Yes, yes, Nathaniel; you had in mind a symbolical tributary of a river existing nowhere except in your somber imagination." Henry's voice registered complaisance mixed with irony.

"The Sudbury, Concord, Rhine, Danube, Thames—the Yellow River or the Nile—they're all one and the same *here*"—he pointed to his head—"or *here*"—he pointed to his heart—"or wherever it is that fables are made."

"I'm only making sport, my friend, as well you should know," said Henry, cossetting him. "Your prose is very fine."

Henry scratched vigorously at an itch buried in the beard at his throat. I smiled to think what flea would dare.

Mollified, Hawthorne said, "I've been thinking of writing a novel set in Salem, in the early years of the Massachusetts Bay Colony, when our progenitors lived in moral isolation and darkness whose noxious source lay in the ancient European forest."

"You have in mind an allegory?" asked Henry.

"It would be as grim a tale as anything set down by Jacob and Wilhelm, whose forests were also dark and malevolent."

"You worry too much about your ancestor John Ha-thorne—a pyromaniac worse than any 'woods burner.' He liked to see poor women burn."

"Thou shalt not suffer a witch to live," I said to myself, quoting Scripture.

"Perhaps," replied Hawthorne, who seemed to be smarting, as though Henry's words had drawn blood. "It was the general delirium of the times."

"If a tale can be made of such repellent doings, you are the man to attempt it—or else that other martyr to the grotesque Edgar Poe."

Henry had read me Poe's "The Pit and the Pendulum," and I had recognized in the prisoner's torments something very like my own. Men are never so ingenious as when they are devising another's pain.

"There will be a minister who disintegrates in that settlement on the edge of nothingness, a man beset by human desire and shame," mused Hawthorne. "At the center of the village where he suffers his martyrdom to sin is a jailhouse and a gallows. . . . I can't see any more of the story than that."

You ought to visit Fenda Freeman, though her gift has faded. The thought of her put me in mind again of the woman I would meet and lie with in Adam's Woods, according to prophecy. I almost believed it. I must have looked strange or at least distracted, because Henry asked me if anything was wrong.

"No," I replied, swatting a pesky fly.

"We are counting on you to angle up our supper," he said.

"Nothing's biting but the flies."

I lifted the string out of the water and saw a hook naked of any worm, and so did Henry, whose eyes glinted wickedly.

"You've been woolgathering!" he chided.

"Let the man alone," said Hawthorne. "He's not your—"

The word *slave* or *nigger* hung in the air like a ghost that cannot be exorcised.

Henry cleared his throat with that *ahem* he was liable to in times of discomfiture.

At that moment, standing foolishly on the shore of Fairhaven Bay, *I did not know how to be*. It is a simple sentence whose words are quickly, even carelessly said. But it is, perhaps, the most important admission to pass one's lips or through one's mind during a lifetime of utterance. The world may turn on it, I think; it may be the pivot and the fulcrum by which all things move. The answer—for it begs a question—determines the direction of the great moral tide that is in ceaseless motion within us and also without us. Jeroboam did not know how to be. Emerson and Garrison knew how to be—Hawthorne, too, I think. Henry was still finding his way. His nature was rougher.

Today, I can admire Henry, but in 1846, he often confused me. I was too habituated by my past to entertain thoughts that were not smoothed by the iron of conformity. Emerson said famously, "A foolish consistency is the hobgoblin of little minds." What are the mass of men and women, whose minds are small, to do? How are we to be when great minds bid us act this way or that, think one way or another, according to their lights? In our fear and littleness, we cling to our hobgoblins.

Ahem . . .

Having cleared his throat, Henry said, "Samuel, why not explore the cliffs on your own? The view is magnificent: You can see Mount Washusett forty miles off. It will do you good to get off on your own and away from all this *talk*."

Talk—miasma of the intellect, a pastime as useless as a child's game of hide the slipper or snap the whip.

Hawthorne had already taken the pole from me and was striding amid cardinal flowers growing near the shore.

"Give me a fat worm, and I guarantee to raise Leviathan."

I left them to their comedy and walked across a bog meadow of English grass toward the uplands, feeling—I am almost embarrassed to admit—an expectation akin to the lustfulness that sometimes comes over every man and beast.

Perusing an atlas belonging to Emerson, I had seen the Congo River winding like a snake across the page. I had been fascinated by it and had felt an inexplicable satisfaction.

"Only the Amazon is mightier," said Emerson then.

I had just carried an armful of wood into his study for the fireplace, and I did not know what he meant by this lesson in geography.

"The name Congo derives from Kikongo, the language spoken by the Bantu people, who live in the vast forests of West-Central Africa," he said thoughtfully. "Kikongo was spoken by many of the slaves brought to the Americas."

Emerson smiled almost beatifically before closing the atlas. I laid the wood on the grate and left him to his thoughts.

With the Sudbury at my feet, I thought that I understood the meaning of his lesson and of my own satisfaction in seeing his finger trace the course of the great river. The Sudbury and the Concord, what were they next to the Congo? What were the Penobscot, Hudson, or Ohio rivers next to it? In America, only the Mississippi was lengthier. And what of the Bantu people who dwelled on the Congo's shore and within its immense basin? If, in his imagination, Hawthorne could walk from Fairhaven Bay to Germania, could I not travel from the bay to the Congo in mine? The thought was more breathtaking than the view from Fairhaven Hill, which Henry had recommended as an antidote to my sullen discontent.

I watched the two of them in the distance: Hawthorne fiddling with the cane pole, raising Leviathan in his head, while Henry skipped stones. I saw myself commandeering the boat and pressing them into a gang of two to row me across the Middle Passage in reverse. I imagined a clockwork adjusted by the hand of God or the Great Artificer so that time flowed backward, and, as it did, the present shed its hours like rain from a wet dog, until the past became contemporary. There, on the banks of the Congo, beneath African oak, red cedar, and mahogany trees, I spoke Kikongo with a Bantu woman, whose skin was black and soft like night, ate the fish of the river where, at evening, white rhinoceros and buffalo bathed. My hand grown back, I caressed her and fathered children who would never know the fear of the auction block or lash. I sent Henry and Hawthorne home to wintry and austere New England, to their books and their talk of books and to the tea parties of the Transcendentalists, and I was myself at last. At last, I knew how to be.

Is that what you want, Samuel? That fatuous dream of

Charles Mercer and his American Colonization Society. To go back to Africa and take up the old life again?

But it was not my old life; it was that of some progenitor laid down in the hold of a ship like firewood or fish to be burned and eaten in the New World. What was Africa to me? Who was I to take satisfaction in its ancient rivers? Who was I to speak Kikongo to the Bantu? For the first time, I thought about my relation to the country in which I had been born and raised, albeit a slave.

Did I hate America? Did I love it? One loves an organ in his body that behaves sweetly and detests it if it should become diseased. Regardless, the organ is his; it belongs to him. Just so does America belong to me in spite of its sickness. Do you think that the parrot in a cage or with a shackle on its leg dreams of the Amazon? I think it dreams of the sky just outside the window, and, if only the cage door or the shackle would open, it would be content to live in the nearest tree, no matter if it grew in Adam's Woods, Boston Common, or the Bowery.

I saw that my bed had been made, though not by me. Like it or not, I was— Well, I would not have said an American. A slave—a person "indentured or apprenticed for life," as our duress was sometimes quaintly called—was not one of the people. A slave was counted as three-fifths human for the purpose of taxation and representation in Congress. I was not an American, but America was the place where my life was being lived. Once, I had looked out from my prison and yearned to be in the stand of trees between Jeroboam's plantation and the river—dreamed even more keenly of being on the river, heading north. Now

I was north, standing on a cliff above Fairhaven Bay, fed by the genteel Sudbury, looking down at what might be two lights of the age, or two lunatics, wading in the shallows with their trouser legs rolled up, while the boat, tied to a sunken dwarf willow, sat on the gravel beach like a child's rendering of Leviathan—or what a fanciful imagination such as Hawthorne's would have raised into sunlight.

I left the cliff to the birds and the wind; I left Henry and Hawthorne to their prattle and play. I walked through alders and maples and into the chestnut, hickory, and pines of Adam's Woods. The way darkened beneath the sylvan canopy. I felt alone and happily so, although a part of me hoped to find there a woman who would fulfill Fenda Freeman's prophecy. I walked with increasing expectations for an hour or more, tripping on sumac bushes and creeper vines in my distraction. But I met no one—not a man, woman, child, or dog—during my aimless ramble.

My expectations defeated, I sat beneath a juniper tree, enjoying its spicy odor. The woods were lively with the movements of birds and small animals that, finding in my life no threat to theirs, went about the business of foraging, nattering, and choiring. I wondered if they entertained ideas of happiness and usefulness, or if those were beside the point of their existence. If they were beside it, what, then, was the point? Unlike the industrious citizens of Concord, be they endowed with superior or ordinary minds, my own existence seemed to have no point at all. I could see little hope for the titmouse or the rabbit.

At another time, I would meet a woman and lie with her—not in Adam's Woods, but in the old Lincoln graveyard, near the unmarked graves of British grenadiers cut down by Yankee musket balls during the famous retreat. She was named Zilpha, the linen spinner and "Black Circe" of Concord. She acknowledged neither future nor past time, but relished, with avidity, the present hour, which she undertook to fill with pleasures that would have shocked the good ladies of the village. Zilpha was too joyous to condemn, and her pleasures were hardly vices, except in the jaundiced eyes of the pious. There was no love between us—Fenda foresaw that aright in the barley grains and candle wax. We came together only twice, but I glimpsed qualities in the depths of her soul such as might have belonged to a trout: quick-wittedness, grace, a kind of majesty, and a pretty shimmer.

I wish that our congress—to be nice—had not been in a graveyard. I worry that my story will be disbelieved, its truth dismissed as the fantasy of yet another literary striver hoping to turn inauspicious ground into a symbol and his life into a fable. If I had been born someone else—a white man of means and a formal education, a person not necessarily of any distinction, but one rooted in the earth on which he treads, as I had never been—if I had not been born a slave, I, too, would be suspicious of this reminiscence.

Being with Zilpha had not been the revelation I had wished. I might have been a fly lighting on a piece of meat for all the joy I took in her. She took the matter lightly, as she did most things the world treats with solemnity. When we had finished our coupling, she laughed good-naturedly. I felt insulted and turned away from her.

"You're too serious!" she scolded. "If you didn't have fun, it's your own doing."

I had known no more of desire than a gelding does. Sadder still, I knew next to nothing about love. Whom, in my twenty-three or twenty-four years, had there been to love? I could not recall a mother, father, or any other close relation. I had had no Jonathan or Patroclus and had never touched a woman before Zilpha took me in her dusky arms. Not that I was innocent, as children often are, of amorous scenes. I had never been a child, any more than I had been a man. I had always been a boy. But I had seen a man turn to a woman to ease himself, and I had seen a woman take comfort from a man. Their union had not been like that of animals, nor had it been like that of lovers. Unblessed, they lay on the damp ground, inside a hut worse than any stable, silent and fearful, like thieves breaking into a house.

"You're an old stick, Samuel," she said, smoothing the skirt of her dress.

What kind of stick? Soft like pine or hard like hickory? Had it been blackened by Henry's match, or had it fallen from an ancient oak in the aboriginal forest? Had Alaric used it to sketch a daydream in the dirt outside the walls of Rome? Or was it a stick such as slaves put between their teeth to keep from crying out while they cleaved to each other on the dirt floor where they lay, beside themselves with hopeless, helpless passion? How much of it was love, how much hatred—none could ever know.

In Adam's Woods, I closed my eyes and tried to refuse the questions that were thrown at me—by whom, I could not have said, unless I was my own interrogator. I fell asleep and woke, to find Henry standing over me. He had been careless with his razor. Henry was not vain except of his thoughts and cared nothing for property except for the movable sort that belongs to the mind. The only mirror he owned was three inches in diameter—enough to satisfy himself of his own existence, if not of the symmetry of his beard.

"We thought you'd been taken," he said lightly.

A tremor passed through me. The fear of being repossessed was never allayed, although I did my best to ignore it. I took comfort in living obscurely, far from the slave states and the great cities of the North, where the hunters searched for fugitives. I had my forged papers, but they would not have fooled a slave catcher. I never felt secure and would not until Emerson and his friends bought me my freedom. But even now, sometimes . . .

"I fell asleep," I said to Henry as I sat up, half in wonder, half in a stupor.

He gave me a bite of his Saint Michael's pear, as a priest might when offering the Host.

"We saved your lunch, although I regret there will be no fish supper tonight. Nathaniel caught only a tiny perch that Christ Himself could not multiply into dinner. I've little hope for our friend. I left him sulking like Achilles in his tent."

I laughed, feeling inexplicably relieved. I have in this account of my year in Walden Woods presented Henry in an unattractive light. At times, he could be overbearing, but I have wronged him if the reader thinks he was always so. Just as one could never be quite certain of the color of his eyes, his mood was also variable. The weathercock is sensitive to changes in the air, while the clock at rest on the mantel tends always in a single direction, which is death. It is better, then, to be fickle and absurd than dogmatic and fussily correct.

We walked to the cliff edge and stood there admiring the scenery.

"Sunsets are common as dirt," said Henry thoughtfully. I feared an aphorism was in the making, and, in the next instant, he delivered it: "But the most glorious emotions grow in them. Only barren hearts are unmoved by twilight."

The western shoulder of Mount Wachusett was brushed with gold. Bluish shadows sprawled over the meadows that rolled eastward from the river, which a rising wind had already darkened. In Concord, the Unitarian meetinghouse's yellow spire had become a black splinter. At the foot of the cliffs, our boat sat like a beached hippopotamus, and Hawthorne seemed no more than a gray bundle left forlornly on a rock.

"Hallo, Hawthorne!" shouted Henry from our lofty vantage, but he must not have heard him. "He's probably got his nose in Longfellow's new poem, when he should be opening his pores to this miraculous light—all the more miraculous because it isn't in the least rare or kept out of circulation by bankers."

I felt adrift. Night was seeping from the rocks and soon would gather its shadows like a tide to drown first the woods and then the cliff. And when the cliff had been eaten away by darkness, I would be as a man standing in midair—a ropewalker with neither pole nor rope on which to step out into oblivion.

Henry had taken off his hat and was sitting on a boulder like a man in a pew, charmed by the stained glass.

"A poor man with holes in his pockets can profit by sunsets as well as a rich one with a vault in which to keep his money and, at the last, his poor bones."

I dared not speak my mind. I was doubtful and afraid. I wanted faith but could no more raise it from the depths than Hawthorne could Leviathan.

"'THE INACCESSIBLENESS OF EVERY THOUGHT but that we are in, is wonderful. What if you come near to it,—you are as remote, when you are nearest, as when you are farthest. Every thought is also a prison; every heaven is also a prison. Therefore we love the poet, the inventor, who in any form, whether in an ode, or in an action, or in looks and behavior, has yielded us a new thought. He unlocks our chains, and admits us to a new scene.'"

I was painting the Emersons' fantastical summerhouse, which Henry and Bronson Alcott had built for them at Bush. Emerson had been reading aloud to Lidian from an essay he had written several years before. He intended to refer to it in a lecture he was to give at Freemasons' Hall. Lidian, who deferred always to her husband in matters of philosophical expression, had become lost in the thicket of his thought. Listening to him reason on the poet's task, I, too, had caught my sleeve on a bramble, so to speak.

"I don't understand what you are saying, Mr. Emerson,"

she said from the shadow of her coal-scuttle bonnet. Her decorousness extended even to her husband.

"What don't you understand?" he asked.

"What you mean by 'the inaccessibleness of every thought, save—'"

"—*But*, not *save*," he said, with a mild reproof. "The inaccessibleness of every thought *but that we are in*, is wonderful."

"The phrase 'The thought that we are in' puzzles me."

And also me, I said to myself while I liberated a blister beetle from the wet paint in which it had become mired.

"I mean to say that we are—every one of us—locked inside a thought that excludes all others," said Emerson tolerantly.

"Mr. Emerson, dear, the meaning is not clear to me."

I wondered whether or not Lidian addressed her husband with equal formality in their marriage bed and decided that she did.

Emerson emphatically closed his journal, indicating a change of topic.

"Samuel, I've read your account in *The Liberator*. It was very fine indeed."

"Mr. Samuel, I was very much moved when Mr. Emerson read it to me," said Lidian, whose genial spirit no illness seemed able to dampen. "I cried at how much you had suffered."

I thanked them both.

"I have heard from Mr. Garrison," said Emerson. "He reports that your narrative produced a great effect in his readers—as much, in fact, as Frederick Douglass's had."

I did not know what I was expected to say, so I said nothing. In a silence magnified by the drone of a wasp, the side gate swung open on its hinges.

"Please excuse me, gentlemen," said Lidian, rising. "I must see to the grocer's boy. Pray he has bought the mutton."

"Mutton!" Emerson grumbled during her retreat to the side gate and her groceries. "You see how the world turns on trifles. The circus of commerce never loses its power to astonish and delight us. Mutton, by God!"

I could not make out whether his grievance was with mutton or with the mundane.

"Mr. Garrison has suggested—and I agree wholeheartedly—that you ought to tell your story at antislavery society meetings held in Boston, Lexington, and here in Concord. You will be doing your people a great service—the Union, too, if reason and honorable debate can lessen the division between North and South and forestall a civil war."

"I am not an orator," I said brusquely, hoping to put an end to the conversation.

"Oratory is not wanted," replied Emerson. "We have enough orators on both sides of the issue to sink the nation under their heavy hearts, leaden words, and ponderous rhetoric. What is needed is the thing itself."

I must have appeared doubtful, for he went on to say, "What is urgently needed is a man who will say plainly and truthfully how it was to be a chattel slave in another man's possession and to have removed himself at the risk of his life."

Is this, then, what I am meant to be? I wondered.

"I would like to think about it, Mr. Emerson."

"Do. Do give some thought to it, Samuel, and give us your answer when you've made up your mind one way or the other."

He stood, tucked the journal under his arm, and walked off toward the house—to see to the mutton, perhaps.

I finished my painting for the day and, putting aside my bucket and brush, went home to my— call it a house. I was tired of living in shacks. Henry was welcome to his, but I would call mine by a more spacious and auspicious name.

"Why am I so cross-grained, so unable to enjoy my new freedom, no matter that I had made myself a present of it?" I said to the dusty bleeding hearts growing in my dooryard. Self-pity can be a spice for our daily meat—for our ration of mutton and bitter ale.

V

ater that summer, Henry went to jail. Sam Staples, who had offered to pay his poll tax, walked sheepishly beside him, past the poor farm, the poorhouse, across the Mill-dam, and into the Middlesex jailhouse. Henry took possession of his second-story cell like a dog a manger or, better said, a doge his summer palace. For subjects, he had only one: a "barn burner." He, too, had been careless with the god's gift to humankind, which Heraclitus deemed the soul's chief constituent, together with water, the baser part.

That night, a drunkard in the cell below Henry's called on the darkness to answer a question.

"What is life?"

The night gave no answer, so the questioner provided one: "So this is life!"

"What is life?" he asked again, and, after a silence, once more replied, "So this is life!"

"What is life?"

"So this is life!"

"What is life?"

"So this is life!"

The drunkard examined the night like a witness in the dock, but the night had no answer for him—not having seen any more than the sot did of what lay inside the heart's darkness, or else being unwilling to disclose it.

The tedious litany continued for some time, until Henry called out to him in exasperation, "Well, what *is* life, then?"

Neither the drunkard nor the night made reply.

Henry had been searching for the answer since his Harvard days. He had looked for it in books, in the wilds, in conversation with Emerson, Channing, Fuller, Alcott, Hawthorne, and his brother, John. Never having found it, did he stand by his cell window or with an ear to the floor, straining with every particle of his being to hear what a drunkard would say? For a moment, did he have the greatest of expectations of finding the answer to philosophy's fundamental concern in the Middlesex jailhouse, on a hot July night in 1846?

Giving no more thought to his place in the universe than a badger would, the barn burner began to sing "Jesus, I My Cross Have Taken." I sometimes wonder whether simple men might not be nearer the truth than the titans among us, if only they had the ambition to speak it.

I remember standing outside the jailhouse that night and calling as loudly as I dared to the barred window of his cell: "Henry, Henry Thoreau." I could see Sam Staples in his house across the alley from the jail, sitting at his supper table. Fortunately, he did not look up from his plate.

The silence seemed absolute—deaf as I was in my nervousness to the noise of crickets, night birds, mosquitoes, creak of branches, and the occasional restless nickering of a horse. To have raised my voice in order to be heard would have shattered the night like a pane of glass, or at least it would have shattered my strained nerves. The moment brought back for me the fear and stealth of nights when I would creep outside into the dark rather than use the common straw and—later—nights spent on Ragged Island, sick with fever, during my flight from Master and Mistress Jeroboam's South.

"Henry!" I called up to the window once again.

He had not heard me. He might have been praising the virtues of temperance and a natural life to his companion; he might have been turning over the thoughts that he would later spin into a famous essay on his imprisonment. More likely, he was asleep. He had had a busy day. He had left his hut in the afternoon to have a shoe mended in the village and had gone to jail instead—carried there by his philosophy and bravado. Henry had gone to jail and would come out more or less the same Henry. In my opinion, conversions do not happen overnight. I believe in a Darwinism of gradual change in the mind as in nature and not in the burning bush or lightning bolt. The road to Damascus leads to Damascus. Henry's night in jail had been a gesture—although not an empty one, I'll grant him that.

The next day, Sam Staples released him. To give the rebel his due, Sam had to evict him. A veiled woman, who might have stepped from a Romantic novel into plain-speaking Concord, had paid his poll tax for him.

"Henry, if you will not go of your own accord, I will put you out, for you cannot stay here any longer," said Sam, tired of Henry's shenanigans.

Henry left his fellow prisoner to finish his own sentence, and, having caught and saddled his horse, was soon gathering huckleberries on Fairhaven Hill.

His imprisonment had been another experiment. He enjoyed it too much for it to have impressed me, though the world celebrates it as a brave act of civil disobedience. Emerson was right when he wrote to him afterward:

> Don't run amuck against the world. Have a good case to try the question on. It is the part of a fanatic to fight out a revolution on the shape of a hat or a surplice, on pædo-baptism, or altar-rails, or fish on Friday. . . . The state tax does not pay the Mexican War. Your coat, your sugar, your Latin & French & German book, your watch does. Yet these you do not stick at buying.

Furious, Henry threw the letter into the fire. When he strode off on his short legs like a field marshal to the barricades, I filched what was left of it.

I never discovered the identity of the mysterious woman who had paid his tax. Many women admired Henry's mind; few, however, saw in him the requisite material for a husband, much less a lover. He was not handsome. Hawthorne was handsome; so, too, was Emerson. Henry had been roughly made. His brows were too beetling, his eyes too sunken, his legs too short, his arms too long, his shoulders too slumped. His clothes were out of fashion, and his manners belonged to a galoot rather than a gallant. He would not have graced a drawing room or a lady's parlor. I could not picture him in a woman's bed. When he danced, as he sometimes did after singing "Tom Bowline," his favorite air, his big feet rode roughshod over his poor partner's toes. An awkward figure in society, he could be seen to best advantage in his hut, in the woods, in the taverns of Concord, and in the Middlesex County jailhouse, where his reputation was made as much as it would be in the lyceums. He would turn his brief but glorious imprisonment into literature. Was this alchemy no better than a forger's art? Was the use to which Henry put his action a kind of profiteering? His fellow citizens considered the night he spent in their jail in no more favorable light than his having burned down three hundred acres of Concord woods and very nearly their town. Those who did not know him might have mistaken him for a fool. But for all his misadventures, Henry could be kind, especially to children, who loved his antics and his stories.

When Henry left his cell, he was not a changed man so much as a chastened one. After that night, he would be more alert to the concerns of ordinary men. We live in the natural world, which was his constant study, after all, although I swear there is no more unnatural creature than a man. Certainly, there is no more cussed one. The following week, he lent his front yard to the Concord Female Anti-Slavery Society.

"Henry, you've become a 'come-outer,'" said Emerson, who had come out for abolition two years before.

"I'm afraid that our efforts will be like those of a man who sets out to save a gnat from drowning and, in the process, squashes it," replied Henry soberly.

"We can only try," said Emerson.

"I fear for the gnat," said Henry.

Is he talking about Nat Turner and his catastrophic uprising? I wondered.

Why it should have taken Emerson so much longer to come out than Garrison or John Brown could be construed as a measure of his mind's fretfulness—the solemn debate he needed to have with himself before a decision could be made. He might change his mind, but not lightly. Henry could be as impulsive as a water bug, but his mentor was a rock on which great causes could dash themselves to pieces while he deliberated their merits. There was no saxifrage that could crumble the mountain of his opinions and beliefs save one: reason.

The meeting in Walden Woods had been publicized in *The Liberator* and other antislavery papers of the time. The Transcendentalists turned out like a fraternal order. Garrison arrived with Lewis Hayden, who had once belonged to Henry Clay, a senator from Kentucky. Hayden was a great man and a brave one. After he had spoken movingly of his life, I made my way to the front of the crowd and, clearing my throat as emphatically as Henry was wont to do, asked Garrison if I might not also tell my story.

"By all means, Mr. Long! I dare say there is hardly a soul here who has not read your narrative in *The Liberator*, but to have it from your own lips would be a privilege."

"Bravo!" shouted Emerson, standing beside Lidian, who encouraged me with a warm smile and a nod of the head.

I sought Henry's gaze to see what emotion it might convey, but his eyes were hidden in the deep sockets of his face. Hayden and I shook hands with the solemnity of two mourners at a funeral while the abolitionists applauded. We might have been congressmen, heroes of a hard-fought campaign, or a pair of talking monkeys.

I repeated what I had told Garrison and his scribe in Boston, although not so readily. I stumbled over my words, as if the consonants had been boulders in my path. I kept the article that reported on the meeting, which appeared in the *Middlesex County Republican*. Its editor, William Schouler, was generous in the space he allocated to my recollections. I will spare my readers their reiteration and supply only the introduction for their curiosity.

ABOLITIONISTS GATHER IN WALDEN WOODS,
CONCORD, FIRST OF AUGUST, 1846.
MR. EMERSON & MR. GARRISON, OF BOSTON,
ADDRESS CROWD.
STIRRING ACCOUNTS OF CRUELTY GIVEN
BY FORMER SLAVES!

Abolitionists and sympathizers came to Walden Woods on Saturday last to attend a meeting of the Concord Female Anti-Slavery Society, presided over by one of its founders, Miss Prudence Ward, of that town. Mr. Ralph Waldo Emerson, eminent moral philosopher, poet, lecturer, and essayist, together with Mr. William Lloyd Garrison, famed abolitionist and publisher of *The Liberator* newspaper, each delivered an address from the front porch of Mr. Henry Thoreau's cottage. Also a resident

of Concord, Mr. Thoreau is a naturalist, an author
of many essays, and the inventor of an improved
pencil, manufactured by the family business of J.
Thoreau & Co.

Two former slaves, Mr. Lewis Hayden, now
residing in Boston, and Mr. Samuel Long, pres-
ently of Concord, spoke with natural eloquence
and the fervor of men who have undergone the
severest trials under the execrable institution of
chattel slavery.

The sky above Concord was gray and gloomy,
suitable for so grave an occasion, and a light rain
fell intermittently on—

I do not remember its having rained that day, but I do
recall that, after Hayden and I had testified to our former
abjection, a party of soldiers marched into Henry's yard,
accompanied by a drum and an old senile dog belonging to Hartwell Bigelow. A sergeant of infantry stood in
the doorway and, with a scarcely perceptible seesawing
on his boot heels, fulminated against the Mexicans with
the vitriol of Jonathan Edwards denouncing sin or Father
Mathew the evils of strong drink. That the soldiers exuded
an atmosphere of spiced gin was beside the point. How so
intemperate an interruption of that most sober of convoca-
tions should have been neglected by the *Middlesex County
Republican* is inexplicable, unless it did not happen on the
day of the abolitionists' revival meeting, but on some other.
Who knows but I might have imagined it while soaking

in a redolent atmosphere of my own making, snug in my hermitage. Memory is partly fact, partly fumes.

And yet, I do remember Henry's glowering. . . . Well, Henry often glowered, and, just as often, smiled like anybody else. At the end of the day, the Henry Thoreau who materializes from the pages of this book will be *my* Henry. There were as many Henries as there were people who held opinions of him. The same will doubtless be true for Samuel Long. People are not truths—we are not even facts. We are atmospheres no easier to catch than a flea or weigh than a gnat. We treat one another like stones able to be grasped by the hand and put in our pockets, forgetting the holes in them.

After the meeting, which had been routed by soldiers or rain or had come to an end in the ordinary way by having exhausted the matter at hand, Hayden and I walked under the chestnut trees to the Emerson house on the Cambridge and Concord Turnpike. I became aware of him as a man. He wore his hair cropped, and his beard and mustache were neatly trimmed. He had the smell of stale tobacco and wintergreen about him, along with a faint odor of sweat in his clothes. Manager of a Boston haberdashery, he outfitted himself with garments that were almost fashionable. While he had endured much in his youth before escaping from Kentucky into Canada, only his eyes told of his suffering—I never saw his naked back or shoulders. I was surprised to hear him grumble about his lumbago. The complaint seemed trivial for a man whose catalogue of misfortunes rivaled Job's—a splinter in the foot of a condemned man limping to the gallows. The ardor with which he had addressed the crowd had been dampened: He was becoming like a coal that has given up its light and heat. But to my eyes, Hayden possessed the particulars of character that make each of us an individual. Sauntering along the dusty road, we were two men together, content to speak or to keep silent as we liked.

After a wordless interval, he said, "Will you be staying on in Concord, Mr. Long, or moving north?"

"I have no plans," I replied.

"You must be cautious. Do not believe for an instant that you are safe."

"I don't."

"I continue to be wary even now that I have my papers."

I tasted the gall of a momentary resentment, because he had papers and I had none but a forgery.

"You must make yourself useful, Mr. Long." To my questioning look, he said, "To Mr. Emerson and Mr. Garrison. If you can be a tool for their purpose—which is a noble one—they may reward you with your freedom."

I almost asked if it did not mortify him to be the tool of others—regardless of the cause—but I thought better of it.

"General Lafayette tipped his hat to me when I was a boy," he said. "If I was worthy of a great man's respect, I am worthy of that of lesser men. We *are* men, Mr. Long, and we should feel neither shame nor inferiority. We cannot help but feel afraid, for our enemies are many and cruel and our protection is nonexistent, but we must swallow our fear as we have had to swallow so much else in life."

In the Emersons' front parlor, where the Concord Female Anti-Slavery Society and the Transcendental Club had assembled, Hayden seemed to grow vague, while I felt empty and wooden, as if I had been hollowed out by termites. I do not know why I should have felt this way. We were not ignored; we were treated like guests. Emerson, Garrison, and the rest were all smiles and compliments. I do not recall if Henry was there. While we were being fussed over, I could not rid my mind of the feeling that Hayden and I were two blue-ribbon oxen at a county fair.

The conversation traveled along the rails of propriety, as it applied to subjects hallowed by the recognition of their import. None dared laugh or smile, except in the beaming manner with which we indicate our approval of others. After a time, Henry—so he *was* there!—grew merry, as he often did in front parlors when high spirits plucked at his sleeve, which they would at unlikely times. He sang a comical song, and then he danced in that clodhopping way of his. Emerson, Garrison, and the rest looked dismayed until— spurred by Henry's example or by the wish to save him from embarrassment—Hayden got up and danced, lumbago and all. Before my wondering eyes, he once more took on shape and substance. I wished that I might take his hand again to confirm his reality and to convey my admiration.

I might have said to him, "You have my respect, sir."

He might have replied, "If it is freely given, I am pleased to have it."

"I see in you an example of how to be a black man living in a world where we are not wanted."

"Do not mistake this caricature for the thing itself."

"'What kind of resistance you had better make, you must decide by the circumstances that surround you, and according to the suggestion of expediency,'" I might have said, invoking Henry Garnet's "Call to Rebellion." But I did not. Our exchange was supposititious and for my mind alone.

The party having been brought to an end by the impending arrival of the Boston stage, Hayden was carried out the door in a flood of well-wishers and into Emerson's shay.

I WALKED TO BRISTER'S HILL to be among my own people. I had avoided the hill, telling myself that it was not on the way to anyplace I happened to be going. The truth lay in the disquiet I had felt when visiting Fenda's shack: a disquiet closer to disgust. Walking the dusty path that wound among shanties and chicken yards, my gorge had risen at seeing once again scenes familiar from my childhood.

Its being Sunday, most of the people on the hill were at church. It had been built of pine boards, with a shake roof, and with the expectation of paint and a modest steeple, but the collection basket had not garnered enough coins to pay for adornments. Still, the roof had been washed by rain, the walls (two of them) bleached by the sun, the floorboards scoured by river sand, and the benches dusted by the worn seats of the faded clothes of the brothers and sisters in Christ. A plain altar and a wooden cross, with a suffering Jesus carved in hickory, were all that set the room apart from a grange hall. And yet, as I listened to the exhortations of the preacher and the fervent *Amens* of his congregation, I sensed that something of glory clung to the bare walls like invisible tendrils of ivy, and I could almost see the Holy Ghost descending on a slant of light.

I had not thought much about religion since I was a boy being "read over" with the other house slaves by Mistress S— in her second-best parlor on Sunday mornings. The blessings of the Savior were not for us, and heaven, if we were ever let inside the gate, would be just another plantation. Henry's and Emerson's relations with the next world were subtle and complicated. Neither man would set foot inside a church, unless it was to see someone off to holy wedlock or eternal life. I doubt they believed in the latter—not as Sunday schools teach it. They had their own ideas about the former, as well. Lord, deliver us from eccentrics and fanatics! No, I had not had much to do with hope and glory.

That day in the African Baptist Church, on Brister's Hill, we sang an old hymn that the masters and overseers would have paid us with the lash for singing, if we had dared:

> Didn't my Lord deliver Daniel?
> Deliver Daniel, deliver Daniel?
> Didn't my Lord deliver Daniel,
> And why not every man?

I had intended to slink home to my cabin after the service, but the congregation eddied around me like an affectionate tide carrying me out the church door. For an instant, I thought I would be borne along, down the hill and into the Sudbury, to have my sins washed clean while the choir sang "We Are Going Down Jordan." I got as far as a deacon's dooryard, where a red rooster was picking at the ground as if the Almighty had seen fit to scatter it with seed pearls.

"Sir, we'd be pleased to have you to supper with us," said the deacon, whose name was Cato Robbins.

Warily, I accepted his invitation. I was unused to the hospitality of negroes, who, as slaves, had neither houses, chickens, nor extra plates to lavish on guests. In fact, I could not recall, as I stood dithering in the Robbins's front yard, ever having been entertained by a black person, except as one slave would share with another a jar of corn liquor doled out on Christmas day by their master to make them grateful.

"Give me your hat, Mr. Long," said Robbins when we had crossed the threshold.

He hung my hat on a peg, and then, rubbing his calloused hands together, he asked me to sit in the best chair. I could hear his wife moving about in the shed, where the stove was. She was cheerfully humming "Didn't My Lord Deliver Daniel?" while, one by one, shelled peas rang into a pot.

The Robbins's two-room house was little better than my own ramshackle place. It was, however, clean and tidy, and the walls had been whitewashed. A rug, stitched together of once-colorful rags, seemed more like a flag of defeat than a bold show of defiance against the general dreariness—relieved, in part, by cheap engravings of a Holy Land without negroes, which had been distributed by the Baptist Missionary Society.

"You visiting, Mr. Long? Have you got people on the hill?" asked Robbins.

"I live down by the village."

"What wouldn't I do for a nice piece of bottomland? This godforsaken dirt would likely kill a mule if a man had a mule to kill. I know it's killing me," he said with a laugh. "We be that much closer to God's heaven than folks living down below, but, Lord, it is a hardscrabble life!"

"Bless us, Jesus!" his wife sang out from the kitchen.

"I have a bean field," I said, somewhat bending the truth.

"Do you now? Beans must just about grow themselves down there!" he said with an envy I enjoyed. "Well, we must all be glad to have work to do in the vineyard."

"Praise Him!" said Mrs. Robbins while she set out the supper.

We made a meal of corn mush, fatback, and peas, which we ate on mismatched plates. The food was good, and the Robbins's faces were kind, but I am ashamed to recall that I looked down on them as simple folk without an ounce of wit or intellect. While I can claim a small measure of both now, I possessed neither quality then. I pitied the Robbinses the triviality of their conversation, which took in the weather, the preacher's remarks, the shabbiness of Lester Ingraham's Sunday coat, the Robbins boy's sprained thumb, the girl's suitor, the health of the chickens, and a fried-fish supper held at the church the weekend before. Not a word was said about the Mexican War or the previous day's antislavery meeting, which they had not attended.

None of the negroes living on Brister's Hill or along the Great Meadows, where a second colony had been established after Massachusetts had outlawed slavery in 1783, had been present in Henry's dooryard.

"I did not see you yesterday at the abolitionists' meeting," I said, determined to throw Robbins into confusion.

He fidgeted, watched a fly on the rim of his plate, and then looked at me.

"I was in the fields yesterday."

"The meeting went on till near sundown. You might have come later to hear Mr. Hayden speak. Mr. Hayden is a courageous man."

Modestly, I did not mention my own contribution to the evening, which, in my mind, had assumed heroic proportions, although, in retrospect, I realize that I had made a poor showing next to Hayden. I have never gotten over my shyness. You would think a slave could not be shy; that such niceties would be no more possible for him than for a sheep or a dog. There is no time or place for privacy on a plantation. But even in a litter of newborn dogs, there will be a runt. I had been the runt of mine.

"Well, you see, Mr. Long, I had the dirt and sweat of the day on me, and I was afraid to give the white folks any offense. There is nothing worse for a man's pride than to watch other folks move upwind of you."

Robbins laughed to prove to me that he had only been joking, but I knew he had spoken in earnest. I, too, had felt the same humiliation. Even so, I sensed that something else had kept him from going down the hill to Walden Woods the day before—something closer to the marrow of the truth. Much later, I realized that the women of the Female Anti-Slavery Society would have welcomed the black people of Concord much as a congress of ornithologists would a flock of birds.

He drank some water—he was, unfortunately for me, a teetotaler. He put the glass on the table, wiped his lips on the back of his hand, grunted, but still he would not speak his mind.

I waited to hear what he might say.

He shifted uneasily in the second-best chair. The ordinary noises of a summer's day—children playing in the yard, two men arguing in the lane, squabbling chickens, a disgruntled crow, a peevish bluebottle—stole into the room with us, but they soon faded into the silence of the familiar.

To provoke him into speech, I said, "White people like to talk about the black man and his troubles."

He replied carefully, like a man refusing alms who might have to beg a crust later, when he was truly hungry.

"We're grateful to the abolitionists and to all white folk who must speak for us because our tongues have been cut out, in a manner of speaking." He was as nervous as if I myself had been a white man. "But the plain truth is, Mr. Long, I feel like a child whenever I see Mr. Emerson. Not that he ain't good to us. He's a fine man. Lot of fine white people in Concord, Mr. Long—no denying it. But . . ."

"But a man gets tired of being the object of other people's goodness," I said, finishing his thought for him.

"He sure does!" said Robbins, pleased that we were in agreement on so delicate a matter.

I did not want to be in agreement with him. I had let myself become ensnared in his feeling of inferiority. I realized that I had been vain of my association, which I thought of as intimacy, with the important men of Concord. Suddenly, I felt like a feudal lord who, visiting the hovel of one of his serfs to show his magnanimity, falls into a dung heap.

"Now, Henry Thoreau is a *fool!*" said Robbins with a horse laugh that invited inspection of his back teeth. "Sometimes, he stops by to visit when he's out rambling. He always brings some little gift: a flute whittled out of a fir branch, a pretty stone picked up out of the river, or a pinecone. Lord knows, if we wanted pinecones, we'd go out and get them ourselves! But he's thoughtful like that and likes to sit in the yard and tell stories. The children love him. Yes, sir, Henry's a sweet fool! I know the man's got sense and education, but he don't show off like some."

I resented Robbins's familiarity with Henry, whom I considered mine. Hadn't Emerson put me in charge of him? Wasn't I paid a stipend every week to keep him from mischief? Henry had showed an entirely different side of himself to this poor, ignorant black—a quality I had not seen before.

"He'll walk up Brister's Hill with a string of perch if he thinks somebody might be hungry for a fish fry."

A book ought not to be a stew pot of gossip and opinions, but that is where the truth lies sometimes, if one has the wit to sift for it.

"You're a friend of his, aren't you, Mr. Long?"

"We're good friends," I said. "You might say I'm his sounding board."

Oh, how readily we will plume ourselves with the merest acquaintance with famous men—or infamous ones if an element of romance attaches to them!

"You don't say!" said Robbins respectfully.

His gaze was fixed on the violet light of dusk seen through the window behind me.

To make sure that he took my meaning, I said, "He likes to try out his thoughts on me before he writes them down."

Thus did I cast Henry's habit of thinking aloud in a light flattering to me. Frankly, I seldom offered him my opinion of his grand ideas, knowing that he would have welcomed it about as much as a flea's. Or so I thought. Maybe he would have been pleased to hear it.

Robbins whistled and said, "A man like him is bound to have trunks full of thoughts."

"He's got a fat ledger book full of them," I boasted, as if I had been its author. "Mr. Channing calls Henry's hut 'the inkstand' because of all the ink he's used up writing them."

"Henry never has a serious word to say when he visits," said Robbins approvingly.

To hear that there was a side to Henry that Robbins had not seen pleased me. I was like a dog jealous of its master's cossetting, unwilling to share it with anyone else even if it meant an occasional beating.

"Mr. Thoreau is mostly serious," I said haughtily. "He's a philosopher and not a clown or minstrel show comic."

"*Philosopher!*" said Robbins with a note of veneration in his husky voice. "To think that the man who plays a wood flute and rolls around on the ground with the children philosophizes!"

Henry had a streak of boyishness running like base metal through the ore of his character. But mostly he was serious. I would watch him pursue the business of philosopher, chasing down an idea and treeing it as a dog does a raccoon or a runaway. I would often see him writing in his journal. For all his seeming indolence and carefree nature, he worked as hard in his hut on his manuscripts and lectures as he did in his bean field or at a barn raising. While he was sociable insofar as he wished to be, he was always ready to lend his strong arm, which his narrow frame belied, and his mechanic's skill to his neighbors' betterment.

"Henry's not a person to lord it over the rest of us. Not like some," said Robbins.

I wondered if he meant me.

His wife—her name, if I remember aright, was Charlotte—came out of the kitchen and sat on what must have been the third-best chair. It was wobbly, like a milking stool with a short leg. She was a pleasant woman in her early middle age. She wore a red rag around her neck, and I wondered idly if it might not have been hiding a scar. Tired, she spread her legs and allowed her dress to drape demurely in a gingham fold between them.

"Supper things all washed and put away," she said.

Outside in the yard, the boy was tormenting a chicken with a stick while, standing by the fence, the girl waited for her suitor, or so I supposed by the pink ribbon in her hair and the way she would rise impatiently onto her toes.

"Another day gone," said the deacon.

"Another day tomorrow," she replied with a woman's unconquerable optimism.

"Lord willing," said the deacon.

The shadows had come out from under the furniture and climbed halfway up the wall while we had been talking.

Robbins began to fidget in his chair. I sensed that the time had come for me to take my leave of them. I did so with the noblesse oblige the feudal lord would have shown if he had not fallen into a backyard shit pile.

Mrs. Robbins eased past her husband's bulk at the front door and stepped out into the yard to examine the darkening sky for omens, as she would doubtless do every day of her life. Her husband's shadow fell on top of hers in a way that made me shiver.

"Come again," called Robbins from his threshold while I started down the hill toward Walden.

I did not think that his invitation was in earnest, and I never stopped there again. I would leave such frolics to Henry, who could afford to be democratic. I had my way to make in the world and needed to be careful of the company I kept. It would do me no good to be considered just another Brister's Hill negro. Henry detested the pious—he called them "goodies." So did Emerson, who was more genteel about it. I did not care for them, either, but I was afraid of their disapproval.

While I walked through the crowding trees, my spirit rebelled. Why should I be always cautious? I asked of the darkness. I don't want to go to church and shout *halleluiahs* and *Amens* or tiptoe around Emerson's study as if it were a flower bed I might trample. I was sick of putting my life in somebody else's hands. I had a hand of my own. It was black, and it wanted nothing more at that moment than to hold a jar of whiskey or to tickle a woman. I wished to be in some low haunt, among worthless, no-account black men for a while.

I plunged down the hill, heedless of tree roots and creepers, eager to destroy the person whom, up until now, I had had little hand in making. There comes a time in a man's life when he needs to hit rock bottom—to be barked like a tree branch, skinned like a rabbit—to be reduced to soup bones by macerating self-pity—to be, finally and entirely, naked as on the day the light first dawned for him. Sometimes there is no better way to begin a reformation than with rioting. To stupefy oneself—to court the sickness unto death—can be of sovereign benefit when one does not know his own mind. Lying in his own vomit, he remembers. He is ashamed, and he remembers.

By Goose Pond, a mulatto named Isaac Till made whiskey. Born in Spanish Town, he had been freed in 1833, when the English abolished slavery throughout the empire. His nose had been cut off by the plantation militia in the Baptist War, as the slave revolt in Jamaica was called. With a bandanna over his nose and mouth, he looked like a highwayman, and indeed his shanty, with a still in the backyard, was called the Highwayman's. The makeshift saloon was condoned by the village as a harmless outlet for negroes. Patrons liked to sit in Till's yard and drink his fiery liquor. One of them might play a fiddle while the rest did a country dance, but mostly they drank, told stories, or pitched pennies.

They had welcomed me until I began to speak. My conversation, having been curried by Henry and Emerson, made them wary. Sitting on a rail fence like a row of sullen blackbirds, they glared at me from bloodshot eyes until Till sent me sprawling with an elbow to the gut. Those on the fence guffawed at my humiliation. Till helped me to my feet, dusted me off, and filled a jar with whiskey "on the house."

I poured it down my throat as if Till had indeed ruptured my gut and it was crying out for an anodyne to ease the pain.

"Ordinarily, we don't care for high-toned niggers, but I see by your missing hand that you have toiled in the vineyard, like the preacher says. So— What's your name?" I told him it. "Sit yourself down, Samuel; we don't stand on ceremony at the Highwayman. Sit down and take your mind off your feet."

I was prepared to dislike Isaac Till for his pompous and fulsome manner as much as I had Cato Robbins for his slyly obsequious one. I would have gotten up and left, but the whiskey was working through my veins like God's own grace.

"You looking for something at the bottom of that jar—or trying to forget it?"

His bandanna would flutter like a sail spilling wind when he talked; a laugh set it flapping.

"Just trying to get along," I said, unable to decide on an answer to his question.

"That's how it is in this woebegone world. Not fit for a black man or a white one, either. There ought never to have been a sixth day of creation. God should have let well enough alone, and if He'd rested Himself after His labors at the Highwayman's, He'd have forgotten all about His harebrained idea of making man- and womankind. The world would have turned out a damn sight better without us shitting up the place."

As if giving evidence to man's debasement, one of the inebriates vomited into the grass.

I leaned against the rough wall of the shanty, stretched my legs, and sang, "The riverbank makes a very good road. / The dead trees will show you the way. / Left foot, peg foot, traveling on, / Follow the Drinking Gourd."

"You look to me, Samuel, like a man full of troubles," said Till, while the besotted blackbirds perched on his fence rail answered my song with a rude one of their own.

"I am a colored man!" I shouted above their impiety. "And I have been banished!"

"Sweet Jesus!" replied the drunkards as nearly in concert as their addled brains and thickened tongues would allow.

"God sent His fiery angel to cast me out!"

"With fire and sword he chased you out the back gate!"

"Now I am a stranger in a strange land!" I cried.

"Lord have mercy!" the chorus groaned.

"The cup is bitter."

"The cup is bitter," they repeated before returning to their jars.

Our lamentation having come abruptly to an end, silence settled over the yard like that which stilled Egypt's houses when the Angel of Death passed over the blood-smeared lintels of the Jews.

I drank a second jar, and, closing my eyes, saw sparks light up the darkness. I heard the sound of pennies being pitched, heavy shoes scuffling, sullen voices rumbling low.

I could have slept there, against the shanty's wall, until the Lord came at the head of His army of the righteous and put us sinners to the fiery sword.

"Samuel. Samuel, wake up!" Not the Lord, but Isaac Till, highwayman, was tugging at my sleeve. It was late; the others had gone home to bed. Though darkness still held sway, it was already Monday morning. "Looks like there's just two colored men of leisure hereabouts," he said.

"I was dreaming," I said, trying to shake off the remnants of sleep.

The moon had sunk low; the stars were unknown to me. I might have been in another country for all I recognized of what lay scattered about in the darkness. The highwayman was leaning over me like a cutthroat. His breath as it came through the cloth of his bandanna smelled of whiskey and something bitter—horseradish maybe. The rims of his ears were edged with the yellow light from the lantern at his back. I noticed that a notch had been cut out of one of them.

"It's gone," I said.

"What is?"

"The dream. There's not even a piece of it left to speak of."

"Better that way. Better not to dream at all." He studied my face in the feeble light. "What's your story, then?"

I did not feel like telling mine again, so I borrowed bits and pieces of Lewis Hayden's, the one I had heard him tell at the abolitionists' picnic. I could just as well have used Joseph's—or Frederick Douglass's. The particulars might be different, but the sorrows were the same.

"You're lucky to have escaped with all your parts, except for your hand," said Till when I had finished Hayden's tale, which I had embroidered with strands of my own to account for my dismemberment. "Most don't, and those who do aren't safe till they got their freedom papers."

I nodded, and for the second time that night, I felt a chill.

"The king of England took my nose, and I still feel like I'm sitting on a woodpile waiting for somebody to come along with a Lucifer match. I want to get up into Canada, where the man hunters can't touch me."

A feeling of enmity for all white people—man hunters and moral philosophers alike—swept over me, so that my head reeled and I was sick. That a man's life should depend on a piece of paper was intolerable.

"Too much 'corn,'" said Till with a smile that neither mocked nor condoned my folly.

He went inside the shack and came out with a damp rag. Tenderly, he wiped my face, like a mother caring for a feverish child or a priest administering the last rites. Impulsively, I took his hand and kissed it. Angrily, he pulled his hand away. An emotion can alter with the swiftness of a leaf being turned over by the wind. I might have embarrassed him, or perhaps he had reasons of his own to turn to me in fury, saying, "You get on your way now, nigger! I don't have time for foolishness!" His reasons might not have been known even to himself—I mean to the part of a man that builds walls to keep his neighbors out.

He went inside and slammed the door behind him. I picked myself up and walked into the night, which was not yet ready for dawn. A mist had grown across the stars; the moon was down. Nothing shone except for two unsteady lights, no bigger than candle flames, far off amid the trees— a farmer's house, no doubt. The world was mostly silent, save for the scuffing of my shoes against Walden Road and the indignant beating of my heart.

I was in a rage against myself and everything that was not myself. I was steeped in anger as the trees were in darkness. A bitter anger, a bitter darkness. I wanted to hide my face behind a bandanna and riot in the village's quiet streets. Had I a Lucifer and some punk wood, I would have made a hell of Concord.

Reckless, I ran through the sleeping town and out the Cambridge Turnpike to stand in perplexity outside Emerson's house. In an instant, I had broken a bedroom window with a stone. The noise, abruptly defiant, sent a shiver through the expectant night. I pictured Garrison in Boston, awakened from sleep by the tremor and rising up in jubilation because the slaves had revolted and were massacring their masters under Nat Turner's solemnly approving gaze. I pictured Garrison in his nightshirt, marching down the street, singing "Come Along, Moses."

I crouched behind a box hedge—night lying in pieces around me like shards of smoked glass, or so it seemed to me, whose body quivered sympathetically with the tumult I had raised. I was curious to know how Emerson would behave. Like a philosopher? Like a man surprised in the dark? Would he come to the window and extemporize in Latin on stoicism? Would he shout defiance into the night? Would he shrink in terror beside Lidian in their bed or hide beneath it?

And what should I do next? Should I step from the safety of the box hedge into the light falling from his window and shout my defiance at *him*?

"Now is the day and the hour. Resistance! Resistance! Resistance!" I cried in Henry Garnet's incendiary words.

No, reader, I did not call aloud for insurrection, but only in my mind. But some would say that the willingness to act is all—if not all, the first step. I was not a brave man—not then and not now; I was only a man with the usual virtues and vices. Was Henry any more than I? Was Emerson?

Emerson appeared at the broken window, like a ghost in a nightshirt, holding a candle and peering into the yard. Lidian stood behind him, shivering in her nightdress. I was sorry to have frightened her. Neither said anything. The silence increased, as if every living thing were straining to hear a word of admonition or rebuke. Not a word was uttered. The world exhaled, and the innocent sounds of a summer's night resumed. The candle was snuffed, the shutters were closed, and the Emersons went back to their bed.

For a reason known only to the deranged, my resentment flared into fury. I walked—*strode,* for there was a deliberateness in my gait—toward Walden Woods and Henry's hut. I wish that I could remember the thoughts—sensations, really—that tumbled through my agitated brain. I recall only the sting of a willow branch whipping my cheek while I stumbled through the woods, and the welt that it raised. At this remove in time, I can only guess what I had meant to do when I reached the hut. Break his window?

Henry would have turned my vandalism into an adage: The greatest service a man can do his neighbor is to break his windows and rid his house and mind of stuffiness.

I stopped by Walden Pond, and, like a Roman taking a ceremonial bath before laying waste to his enemies, I washed myself in its dark water. It sobered me and brought down the temperature of my ire. What, after all, had Henry done to me? He had been disdainful at times, impatient, dismissive, even, on occasion, cruel. But he treated everyone—stranger, friend, or acquaintance—the same. He was roughly fashioned and a Jacksonian Democrat. While he could rub people the wrong way, he also delighted them. He lived by no man's sufferance, but by his own conscience and industry. If he was ever a guest, as he had been and would be again in Emerson's house, he was neither obsequious nor indolent.

Chastened, I walked to his cabin and saw that the candles were lit, the front door open to a night that was always kind to Henry. I suspect that he would have welcomed a catamount into his hut and put out a saucer of milk, as though it were no fiercer than a house cat. I sat under the open window and listened to the scratching of his pen against the pages of his ever-increasing journal, thinking, *This is the sound of a mind working late into the night, when the body wishes for sleep but the muted voice natters on. Scratch, scratch, scratch,* like a dog digging at its fleas. I was grateful not to be caught in such toils. I would sooner have mucked out the Augean stables—it was a job I was used to, after all. *Scratch, scratch, scratch.* I pictured the ink laid down by Henry in words, thick as leaves, intensifying the darkness. From the top of a pitch-pine tree, a thrush trilled in expectation of first light.

What makes a man behave so? I wondered. To struggle endlessly against himself as one might try to shift a boulder from his path or rid himself of a stubborn stool. I could see nothing in it but burden and futility.

Scratch, scratch, scratch. The sound no longer nettled me. Now it consoled like the noise made by a guitarist's calloused fingers sliding over the strings, reminding us of human imperfection and tenderness. While I listened to the music of Henry's lucubration, my eyes closed and I prepared to make the "middle passage" required each night of us all until the last, when the light will be put out for good.

I AWOKE LATE IN THE MORNING, to find a blanket covering me and, under a piece of limestone, a note in Henry's sprawling and untidy hand.

> Monday, 3rd August

> Come, if you will, to Emerson's this afternoon. A picnic is being made for Mr. Hawthorne, Inspector of the Revenue, who is treating us to a royal visit. Waldo thinks that you, being one of his few Concord intimates, should be on hand at our little party. Formal dress is not required.

> Your friend, HENRY.

> P.S.
> The night air can be dangerous.

That a man could wish, at one moment, to bite the hand that feeds him and, at the next, to lap up crumbs of another's affection is proof of his insecurity. I doubt that few in Middlesex County were as unsure of themselves and their place among their fellows as I was then. To have been called an "intimate" and to have been signed "your friend" pleased me. With the vanity of an acolyte putting away the stole of the priest he serves, I folded Henry's blanket and laid it on his cot. Thus will a man seek nourishment in thin air and preen himself with feathers and broken buttons if his wits are turned. I would gladly go to Bush, I decided.

After having left the Old Manse, Hawthorne was appointed Inspector of the Revenue for the Port of Salem. While his post in the Custom House relieved the family's pinched existence, Hawthorne worried that the inspiration that had favored him in Concord would not follow him to Salem. During his visits to the village, he admitted to a nostalgia for the "charmed atmosphere" of Concord and the surrounding countryside.

I stopped at my cabin to wash and change into clean clothes, and then I walked out the turnpike I had trod like one of the Furies on the previous night. Passing by the Emersons' still-shuttered window, I was careful to look everywhere but at it. Had anyone witnessed my shifty manner, I would have given myself away as the perpetrator of the night's mischief. Henry was waiting at the gate.

"Lidian and I were treated to a shivaree," said Emerson after Henry and I had shaken hands with Hawthorne and settled ourselves on two slatted garden chairs—comfortable as the rack. "Evidently, they mistook us for a bridal pair. To my eyes, she does retain her bloom and sweetness."

He smiled gallantly at his wife, whose gaunt face managed a ragged blush.

"It's a shame that Mrs. Hawthorne could not accompany you," she said.

"She awoke this morning with another of her sick headaches," replied Hawthorne.

"I am sorry to hear it," said Lidian ruefully, lowering her gaze from his shy face to a bed of yellow violets.

"Were you frightened by the outrage?" inquired Hawthorne.

"Outrage?" said Emerson, nonplussed.

"The window," replied Hawthorne, nodding in its direction.

I thought his use of the word *outrage* to be exaggerated in the case of a broken window. Henry must have thought the same, because he said, "If a windowpane is reason for outrage, what can one say about the Mexican War?"

"There is nothing so alarming as the sound of splintering glass," said Hawthorne, ignoring Henry's contrariness. "One imagines Vesuvius or some other paroxysm of nature."

"Or an insurrection," said Henry, his eyes lively in their deep sockets.

"Smashing my window was not an act of civil disobedience, Henry," said Emerson.

"I fear there are iconoclasts afoot," replied Henry with a smile that took in his little audience before finally lighting on me.

I squirmed, waiting to see if he would betray me. He

kicked at a pebble in the grass but let the matter drop. A mockingbird sang unreliably in the interval.

"I've read that electricity has been successful in the treatment of migraine," said Lidian.

Hawthorne answered her solicitous glance with a grateful one, which was interrupted by Henry's imitation of a sick duck.

"*Quack, quack, quack.*"

"Don't be whimsical, Henry!" admonished Emerson, while Lidian frowned. "*Quack* derives from the Dutch word *quacksalver*, meaning a 'hawker of salve.'"

"That's as may be, Mr. Emerson, but I don't think poor Mrs. Hawthorne's headaches are in the least amusing," said Lidian reproachfully, glancing at Henry.

"No, you are right to be annoyed, Lidian," said Emerson.

Hawthorne shrugged; Henry seemed perplexed.

Will you incriminate me in last night's offense against property to shift disapproval from yourself? I wondered.

"Samuel, will you have time tomorrow to replace the broken windowpane? It is too bad to be shut up when the weather is hot," said Emerson.

"I'll be glad to, sir," I replied, smiling with an agreeable, if a fraudulent, charm.

Henry laughed, seemingly for no good reason. The Emersons looked askance at him.

"Shall we play a game of pall-mall?" suggested Hawthorne to change the subject.

"Oh, yes!" said Lidian, glad of a diversion.

"In his diary, Pepys mentions having seen the game for the first time, played in St. James's Park, during the reign of Charles the Second," said Emerson, taking obvious pleasure—or refuge—in pedantry.

"I'm going after sand cherries," said Henry, rising from his chair.

"I'll come, as well," I said, wanting to be away from there.

"That leaves three to play," said Lidian.

"A sufficiency of ardor is better than a superfluity of lukewarm interest," said Emerson as pithily as if he had rehearsed his remark. He may well have done so in his shaving mirror, while he stropped his razor that morning, and had been waiting for a suitable occasion.

"Well said, Waldo!" Henry shouted as he started across the lawn toward Mill Brook on his short legs—"the legs of a galoot," Henry called them in becoming self-deprecation.

Following after him, I heard Hawthorne's mallet strike the heavy ball with a click.

"To knock a wooden ball through an iron hoop is no good reason to keep one's gaze fixed upon the ground," said Henry. "But to delight in a shell, a stone, or a blade of grass . . . There's divinity in it. Waldo wrote in *Nature*, 'God dresses the soul, which He has called into time.' I think he dresses it in grass. Waldo's chamber hardly needed ventilation, Samuel, no more than his thoughts do. He is the chanticleer of a new morning, while I am only a gamecock digging in its spurs."

I stood with my eyes on the brook, sullenly defiant.

Henry broke into a laugh worthy of a schoolboy who had pulled a prank.

"Whatever your reason, Samuel, it was well done and probably needed doing, if only for your soul's peace."

He squatted beside a low bush and began to pick the ripened purple fruit—one for his mouth and two for his hat. Thus would prudence always outweigh self-indulgence in him.

"I don't know why I did it," I muttered.

"You know perfectly well! But I've wasted enough time on the subject and you, no doubt, in brooding on it. It is too fine an afternoon to rake over yesterday's coals or to put ourselves under an obligation, for courtesy's sake, to send a little ball hissing though the grass toward a dubious end. I'd rather blind man's buff or snap the whip than pall-mall, even if a king of England once played it."

I took off my shoes and washed my dusty feet in the brook. Laying my head on a flat gray rock warmed by the sun, I stared at unraveling clouds, wishing that I might see an angel—or a devil. One would be as good as another to prove an afterlife. Henry joined me and offered me his hat, from which I ate a handful of tart cherries.

A muskrat waddled over the brook's dry margin, disturbing the reeds and tall grass before slipping nonchalantly into the brown water. While Henry had not missed its comical progress, I saw that his mind was elsewhere.

He spit out a pit onto his palm and, showing it to me, said, "To each is given a hard, irreducible core where what is essential to him resides. Some call it the soul, others a man's character. The next time you don't know who you are, Samuel, remember the cherry and its stone."

"Why must you always draw lessons?" I asked petulantly. "Why not let things be themselves?"

It was fine for the seers to have spoken in riddles, for

Jesus in parables, and for His disciples in tongues, but it was a wearisome habit in an ordinary man.

"What can you expect of a pencil maker?" Henry said with a snort of self-derision.

My self-righteousness collapsed, and I laughed.

"Cato Robbins says you're a fool."

"He's right: I *am* a fool." He took a wooden flute from his pocket, piped a merry tune, and danced. "All the wisest men have been so."

He pocketed the flute and headed toward the river and the site of the Old North Bridge. I followed at his heels; he had power over me, fight against it however I might. We stopped at the obelisk erected ten years earlier on the east bank of the Concord, half a mile beyond Egg Rock. The bridge was gone; only the stone abutments remained, spotted orange with lichen. Henry took off his straw hat and mopped his brow with his sleeve. Then he recited Emerson's hymn in a tone of voice whose irony verged on irreverence.

> "By the rude bridge that arched the flood,
> Their flag to April's breeze unfurled,
> Here once the embattled farmers stood
> And fired the shot heard round the world."

"The echoes of that shot can still be heard," said Henry, joining me on the bank. "At the Nueces River, in Santa Cruz, Tucson, and in the Sonoma Valley. Mr. Polk is getting himself a western coast, some copper mines, and God knows what else for America to fatten on. Waldo, of course, got himself a famous patriotic poem."

Henry held with Dr. Johnson that "patriotism is the last refuge of the scoundrel."

I rubbed my hand against the obelisk, relishing the roughness of its granite stones.

"I dislike monuments; they're falsities ossified into a semblance of truth. This obelisk bears the same relation to facts as this morning's coddled egg did to the hen that laid it." He picked up a stone and held it as if it were that egg. "Obelisk indeed! What does Egypt of the pharaohs have to do with Concord?" He gazed at the stone as though he hoped to find an answer there. "I was mostly in earnest when I allowed Sam Staples to jail me. It was a self-important gesture, but it was also a conscientious one. The two can be difficult to disentangle. The truth is, Samuel—since we seem to be concerned with it at the moment—one's motives are seldom pure."

He threw the stone into the water and watched the ripples spread toward the limit of their influence before merging in the river's atoms.

"Why do ripples come to an end?" he asked of the water, since his gaze was on it and not on me. "Because Sir Isaac Newton tells us so? Is it not reasonable to believe instead that they carry on throughout the universe in another form? In Corinthians, we are told, '. . . it is sown a natural body; it is raised a spiritual body.' A corpse is made incorruptible by the action of the spirit, but the principle must apply to all matter—even to a ripple of water: It, too, must enter the rarefied dimension where it can no longer be perceived but exists nonetheless. If only in our conviction."

Bored, I began to play with my jackknife.

"'Instantly it is raised, transfigured; the corruptible has put on incorruption. Henceforth it is an object of beauty, however base its origin and neighborhood. . . . In its grub state, it cannot fly, it cannot shine. . . . But suddenly, without observation, the selfsame thing unfurls beautiful wings, and is an angel of wisdom. So is there no fact, no event, in our private history, which shall not, sooner or later, lose its adhesive, inert form, and astonish us by soaring from our body into the empyrean.' Waldo wrote that somewhere or other—God bless his prolixity."

All of a sudden, Henry looked like a man whose stomach had soured, and, turning his back on the memorial, he said to me, "We think too much."

"What do you think about love, Henry?" I asked impulsively.

In our private, mutual history, I had seldom been bold enough to ask Henry a question whose answer demanded more of his intellect than the plane geometry he used in land surveying, which fascinated me. Subjects like love, regardless of their universality, had seemed beyond my ken.

"I can tell you what the ancients thought of it and the opinions of a few of our modern poets. Their words are grains they happened to choose for their poetical conceit because they made a pretty sound or figure, but I suspect that the grains they overlooked are nearer to the truth of love. In any case, I cannot presume to answer you, Samuel, having no real experience of it."

"Nor have I," I said truthfully, knowing that my encounters with Zilpha had incited in me emotions too simplistic to be called by that most complex of human feelings. "I have had only carnal experience."

"Then you have the advantage of me. I've known neither love's balm nor its tumult, only its fretfulness."

We left the ruined bridge and walked south along the river into the village. At Shattuck's store, Henry bought a bag of barley sugar sticks.

"To rid our minds of the sour taste," he said, handing me one. "A candy to sweeten the garlicky cud of thought."

We wandered through the village. He stopped at the jailhouse and insisted on showing me where he had been lodged, a guest of the county—board included. He took me upstairs to the cell that had been his for the night and pointed out its amenities and lines of doggerel scratched by former inmates on the plastered walls. A man wearing a torn coat was snoring on a cot, while the gold light of evening, barred with shadows, fell across his toothless face.

"I passed a pleasant night here," said Henry, as one might say of a deluxe hotel in Boston or Philadelphia. "I was sorry to leave it."

"Evening, Henry," said Sam Staples, arriving at the top of the creaking staircase with the jangle of keys and of tinware on a tray for the inmate's supper. "Keeping out of trouble, I hope."

"I hope to disturb the peace regularly in this world and—if practicable—in the next," said Henry, smiling broadly at his erstwhile warder.

"Well, see that you don't do it in Concord," said Staples placidly.

We continued on our way, past the bank, the fire

insurance company, and the Unitarian meetinghouse. Henry could not resist making one of the ironic observations of which he was so fond.

"The columns of the Concord Bank are fancy Ionic, those of the Unitarian meetinghouse plain Doric. They both hold up the porch roof."

We passed by the barber's, the milliner's, the haberdasher's, and the blacksmith's. The blacksmith in his leather apron—his face looking scorched as a piece of char cloth—paused in his hammering long enough to denounce Henry as a "woods burner" and a "jailbird." At Mill-dam, Henry stopped to shout a raucous "hallo!" to the coopers. They waved their caps in answer. He clambered down to Mill Pond and discussed a question of bait with an angler whose worm seemed unable to whet the appetite of any fish. Henry and I went as far as Sudbury Street and the Fitchburg Railroad. We followed its tracks southerly, bruising our heels like the very devil on the stones, until we came to Stow Woods.

"Let me pay *you* a visit, Samuel," said Henry, his weather-beaten face hidden in the shadow of his hat.

His visits to my cabin had been few. We walked through the darkening pines, the fallen needles soft beneath our boots, the air redolent of turpentine and clamorous with birds.

I unlocked my front door. Henry held his tongue concerning my attachment to property, my jealousy of things, although there was no property to speak of and certainly nothing to guard. We went inside. He took one chair, and I the other. There was no first- or second-best one. We sat awhile in silence—that is, neither of us spoke; the rumors of a summer's night were borne in to us by the rising breeze, which was conversation enough. Henry took off his boots like a man making himself at home. I took off mine like a man at ease with a friend.

"Are you hungry?" I asked him finally. He was my guest, and, besides the barley sugar sweets, we had eaten nothing since Mrs. Emerson's sandwiches and rhubarb pie. "I have some cheese and bread."

"Thank you, Samuel. I'll take some of both."

Eating allowed us to be silent awhile longer. I did not know whether Henry was saving an observation or polishing an epigram in his mind; he was not usually reticent. While I enjoyed an intermission in what seemed sometimes to be a play without an interlude, I grew anxious, watching the darkness slowly engulf the room. When I could stand the suspense no longer, I blurted, "Was there something you wished to say, Henry?"

"No," he replied without a trace of ill humor or, for that matter, curiosity.

I was puzzled. Unlike Hawthorne, whose mouth might have rusted shut for all the use he made of it, Henry could "talk the ears off a field of corn," as Alcott used to say.

He stood, brushed bread crumbs from his lap, stepped to the window, peered out at the sumac bushes, and sat down again.

"I loved my brother, John," he said wistfully. "Perhaps more than anyone else. It was a great happiness to have him at my side. Our trip on the Merrimack and Concord was the summit of my life. He ought not to have died."

I almost said something, but I realized that I was

overhearing a monologue; that, in my little room made spacious by the night, which tends toward infinity, Henry had forgotten me. He was with his ghosts, while I sat in the dark like a maggot in a tin of meat.

"Why am I fashioned so? I am ugly as Hephaestus at his forge—mine, the writing desk, hands blackened by soot turned into ink, a friend to falsehood. What was God thinking when He created us? Easier to understand a mole than a man! Poor Abiram and his fellow dissenters 'went down alive into the pit, and the earth closed upon them' for their disobedience. . . . George Herbert's 'Easter Wings' . . . 'Lord, who createdst man in wealth and store, / Though foolishly he lost the same, / Decaying more and more / Till he became / Most poore . . .' Lord, deliver us from complications, though we seem to be delivered from one complication to the next. . . ."

Henry's voice rose and fell while he talked. The thread was hard to lay hold of—his reverie obscured by its fitfulness. I fell into a drowse while he droned on. I was sometimes in the room with him and, at other times, adrift among the wreckage of my own memory, like a shipwrecked sailor grasping at jetsam. I remembered having seen a woman naked on the auction block while a man lifted her breasts with a riding crop, then parted her buttocks with it. I had sobbed in answer to her tears of humiliation. She was bought and taken away, and I did not see her again. Was she my mother?

Henry's voice had insinuated itself into my reverie:

"When I was a child, I had a box turtle. It lived in the yard under a red huckleberry bush. It was a pretty thing! I admired its house. My cabin is the next-best thing. . . .

I could cart away my belongings in a trice if the bailiff came knocking. What business would a bailiff have with me? Neither my house nor my self is mortgaged. I owe no one. . . . Except for the mysterious lady who paid my tax and got me put out of my white room. Damn her for her officiousness! I can't abide it in people or in governments. . . . I should have been a box turtle living beneath a berry bush . . . so long as I kept well clear of the soup pot. . . . People will eat almost anything, like the worm its dirt and the mole its worm. . . . While we live, we have our peck of dirt to eat. How much, I wonder, have I swallowed on my way to dusty death? If we could eat our words—what a diet mine or Waldo's would make, forced down the gullets of people who care more for Cartwright's Knickerbocker Rules than for Milton's or Dante's sublime poems! Nothing comical about divinity. . . . To have lived under the old gods' dispensation, to have played the Pan flute in a sylvan glade, far from Eden and sin . . ."

I remembered my first experience of desire. One must have at least a small allowance of freedom in order to covet—to want something more than the daily ration of bread and escape from the lash. What does a horse or an ox covet? We could not even call our skins our own, since they could be striped at another's pleasure. But I had wanted the shiny spoon with which the master's young daughter played in the dirt of the yard.

I was aware again of Henry's voice.

"To read may be more a waste of spirit than watching the Knickerbockers play baseball at Elysian Fields or Hawthorne, Waldo, and Lidian—he calls her

'Queenie'—pall-mall at Bush. We belong outdoors and not in fusty rooms reading musty books. . . . Without John, I prefer to get away by myself. Now that he's gone, I enjoy my own company best. 'To go into solitude, a man needs to retire as much from his chamber as from society. I am not solitary whilst I read and write, though nobody is with me. But if a man would be alone, let him look at the stars.' Waldo wrote that, too. In *Nature*, was it? Emerson's a giant; I'm a pygmy. . . . *Africa* . . . I can't even say the word without shuddering!"

I remembered an ancient slave woman. She had been brought here from the Kingdom of Dahomey when she was a young child. Her mother and she had passed through the "Door of No Return," in the port town of Whydah, and boarded a Portuguese slaver's ship. They were laid in the hold, shackled to each other. Her mother died during the Middle Passage; the girl was left chained to her corpse until it began to stink. To think that the girl's grandmother had been one of King Ghezo's Amazonian warriors!

Henry spoke like one who was confessing.

"I've never understood people. John understood them. He could make them laugh. I can only make them laugh by playing the fool. . . . I'm a clown beating a rustic with a pig's bladder. . . . John had lightness of spirit. . . . I come back to him—I come back to you, brother, always. . . . Circularity is the great principle, although civilization is built on the straight line and the right angle related by geometry. . . . Savage races worship the circle, the moon, the rounded hill, the gravid belly, the full breast, the ocean's curve. '. . . the Concord circling nine times round.'

. . . Man is no better than the mole. . . . Whimsicality. To knock a ball through an iron hoop! With a phosphorous match, I could make a blaze that would light the world . . . and scorch it to its roots. 'Woods burner,' *ha*! . . . Absurd obelisk—what fools men are to ape the ancients! We require iconoclasts and incendiaries, Sam Staples, and I will not stay out of trouble in Concord!"

I remembered sitting all day in a barrel for having taken the little girl's spoon. But first, I had been made to swallow one, two, three spoons of castor oil. Jeroboam called it 'pickling.' I was pickled twice—the second time, for daydreaming. To be put down into the fetid darkness, ankle chained to ankle . . . galling . . . 'Night is the solvent in which matter is dissolved.' Henry said that, or Waldo did, or maybe the madman poet Jones Very, who claimed to be the Second Coming of Christ. There was a large meadow next to Jeroboam's place. They called it "Christian Fields," and the white people would go there on Sunday afternoon and praise God from whom all blessings flow.

"I could walk out your door, Samuel, into the night and onward to the next world."

I opened my eyes on the darkness of the room. Had he spoken to me?

"Did you say something, Henry?"

"I said that night is a magical passage to eternity," he replied with the fervor of an evangelist crusading for lost souls.

. . . the lost sheep, the lost spoon . . .

"We say 'the light of common day' because we acknowledge the extraordinary nature of night."

I could see nothing anymore of Henry, who had succeeded in turning himself into words. He went on, expatiating on night in a veritable rapture. An owl put a word in, but the meaning was obscure. I was becoming impatient.

"What about the field beans?" I asked.

"What can I learn of beans or beans of me?" he replied Socratically.

"They need weeding," I said. "Preferably by the light of common day."

"You are right to remind me," he said. "One world at a time."

I lighted the candles, and the phantasms fled.

Henry unhooked his ankles from the chair legs and stretched his luxuriously. He is just a man after all, I thought as I put away the bread and cheese.

"Tomorrow, we'll go to Shattuck's store and buy a piece of glass and, afterward, to Bush, where I will give you a lesson in glazing."

VI

ENRY HAD READ OF BURTON'S TRAVELS in Arabia, Franklin's in the Arctic, Mungo Park's in Africa, and Darwin's in the Galápagos; travel books were a secret pleasure for the man who boasted, "It is not worth the while to go round the world to count the cats in Zanzibar." But the precincts of Concord, made increasingly smaller by the Fitchburg and its right-of-way, by the hewers of trees and lake ice, by trivial minds and backbiting factions, would sometimes fret him. Regardless of how widely Henry had traveled in Concord, there were times when he yearned to avail himself of the novelties of distance.

"Walden Woods can be a narrow place for a man with seven-league boots," I had once overheard him grumble to a blue heron wading stiff-legged in the shallows of the pond.

The heron gave no reply, being too haughty a creature to concern itself with the humors of our kind. Nature's mute indifference has never stopped a man from apostrophizing a bird or an animal or even the tongue-tied ocean, which, if it could hear, must listen to our lamentations above its own awful roar.

At the end of August, Henry was seized by an urge to travel—"to put distance between Shattuck's tinned meats and my appetite." And so it was that, on September 2, fifty-six miles up the Houlton Road from Bangor, we found ourselves waiting impatiently at Mattawamkeag Point for Louis Neptune and a shabby cohort of Indians. Two days before, on Indian Island, near Old Town, we had arranged with him to meet us farther up the Penobscot, at the point, whence Henry and I would be carried in one of Neptune's canoes on the river's western branch.

Henry and I had come ashore in hopes of finding the Abenaki peaceably smoking pipes in their wigwams. We had found only a remnant of savages, greased with bear fat against the mosquitoes and blackflies. Our Walden huts seemed like palaces compared to those tumbled-down shacks, our clothes finery worn by country gentlemen. The Indians were raggedly dressed in old shirts and pantaloons that had once belonged to Canuck boatmen. Equally tattered but with a regal air, Louis Neptune appeared to be the chief ragamuffin on that small island in the Penobscot.

"God made them noble, and the white man degraded them," said Henry bitterly after we had left the island to continue on our way north along the riverbank.

"At least the moose are as He made them," I replied—sagaciously, I thought, although I had laid eyes on neither.

Henry turned an angry gaze on me and said, "I begin to worry that they, too, will one day be no more than a boy's pretty dream. Better for them that they be forgotten or slaughtered than they fret away their days in a menagerie."

My eyes shied from Henry's, as though his were live

coals. I went down to the water's edge and looked at nothing in particular. I heard him behind me, kicking at stones.

The sawmills we had seen downriver, where white pines were milled into matchsticks, as well as Indian Island's squalor, had soured Henry, but he hoped to discover in the wilderness surrounding Mount Ktaadn the primitive state of the earth's first people. In the granite and timbered heart of Maine, he sought a vestige of the primeval forest that, at the time of the first North American settlements, had been as common as air. The land had belonged to its ancient inhabitants by right of possession, but, careless of law, they had not stopped to acquire the deed to it and, as a result of their negligence, would lose it.

"John and I collected arrowheads when we were boys," Henry had confided during the boat trip from Boston. He had been at the summit of good humor, in anticipation of ascending Mount Ktaadn, whose peak rose a mile above sea level. "I've longed to see the descendants of the people who made them, still living in a natural state, dignified by forests and mountains and unspoiled by the manufactories of things hallowed by neither practical nor spiritual necessity."

We would see nothing of the natural man during our twelve days in the Maine woods. Instead of him, we encountered Louis Neptune and his scant clan of Abenaki; Canuck boatmen; and lumbermen arguing the merits of President Polk's recent declaration of war with Mexico.

For comfort's sake, we spent some nights, like cuckoos, in vacant loggers' cabins, empty of any furnishings save a barrel, a pail, and a basin. We sometimes found greasy playing cards and, once to our astonishment, a pamphlet containing

Waldo Emerson's address on West Indian emancipation. We slept on the soft leaves of the arborvitae tree, which Henry relished for the Latin word's English meaning: tree of life. Brewed, it made a strong cedar tea, employed by woodsmen as a remedy against the aches and pains of hard labor.

"In our rustic bedding, at least, the ancient life survives," said Henry, rolling the aromatic leaves between his palms to release their invigorating odor.

While life as it was lived by ignoble savages and hard men of the Penobscot River Basin might have disappointed him, he took pleasure in the beauty of the way. Besides the arborvitae, spruce, larch, and balsam trees lined Houlton Road, which had been cut through the unincorporated wilderness with immense effort, like every other work of man in his subjugation of savagery. The forest on either side of the road bore no trace of human presence, but only that of deer and moose, bears and wolves, which shrank from ours as one would a plague ship. I did not like this country; to be honest, I was afraid of it and wished myself back in Walden Woods.

Occasionally, the trees crowding the bank would open, like a theater drape, revealing a stage rough-hewn by loggers, where they could roll great trunks down into the water, which was dashing over rocks toward Bangor and Penobscot Bay—and, if they should elude the grasp of commerce, out onto the Atlantic. Sailors would sometimes happen on logs afloat in the sea-lanes, branded with the names of men who had felled them. Amid the arboreal gaps, pigeon woodpeckers came and went, like gossipy playgoers during intermission. On the river, whistler ducks, with black bellies and long red beaks, called *waa-chooo* to one another, a most unmusical sound, like a sneeze following a pinch of snuff. And always above the tumult of the rapids, the chickadee—sweetest bird of all—delighted us with its merry song.

I remember Henry's having read aloud from his journal while we reclined on soft pine needles carelessly shed by a nature that will always be profligate until men flourish their axes and pruning hooks to stunt it.

"'This was what you might call a bran-new country; the only roads were of Nature's making, and the few houses were camps.'" A tremor in his voice betrayed his apprehension. "'Here, then, one could no longer accuse institutions and society, but must front the true source of evil.'"

Does he believe the wilderness is evil? I wondered. Hawthorne seems to have thought so; the forest was where the devil convened its jubilees in some of his tales. The religious in the first settlements were convinced that the unspeakable lay just beyond the ambits of their candles' flames, within a darkness so obscure that not even the good and the prudent could resist a second fall. I think that, for Henry, the evil of which he wrote lay not in the hearts of humankind, but in the principle of wilderness, which is an unchecked rage capable of tearing earth itself apart. It was the evil of a vegetable world that acknowledged no limit to its growth, of the mineral world that strained perpetually to remake the features of the earth, and of an animal world that would, if left ungoverned, let one man or beast tear the throat out of another.

Disconcerted, I declared with the ardor of someone announcing a discovery, "It is a pleasant afternoon!"

"Uncommonly hot for September," he replied, taking off his hat and sniffing the hatband as someone might who wishes to affirm his place among the gross elements.

Henry's prosaic observation on the weather struck me as remarkable: Even a man such as he, I said to myself, can, in a trice, plummet from the aeries of sublime thought to the worn path of the commonplace!

Our trip was not entirely given over to the rigors of mind and body. Much of the way *was* pleasant. We did not always go by shank's mare, but traveled, at intervals, by coach or wagon, canoe or rowboat.

On the western branch of the Penobscot, we stayed briefly with a Kennebec Scotsman named McCauslin, who had built a large house at the mouth of the Little Schoodic. A convivial host, though seldom afforded an opportunity to prove it, he lavished on us luxuries indicative of a genuine hospitality. Henry and I slept on feather beds and dined on shad, ham and eggs, potatoes and cheese, mountain cranberries, white sweet cakes and yellow hotcakes. McCauslin kept dairy cows, and Henry and I buttered our boots against rain and river water. During the rain, which drummed against his shingled roof, we browsed—for reading's sake—among his books. In his scant library were cheap editions of flash novels, Eugène Sue's *Wandering Jew*, Parish's geography, and a volume bearing the lurid title *The United States Criminal Calendar: or, An Awful Warning to the Youth of America; Being an Account of the Most Horrid Murders, Piracies, Highway Robberies*. He also owned several of the Leatherstocking Tales—more to our liking.

James Fenimore Cooper's idea of the ancient forest and its indigenes was at variance with the Almighty's adjuration to the Edenic couple, as expressed in Genesis 1: ". . . and God said unto them, Be fruitful, and multiply, and replenish the earth, and subdue it . . ." Like William Bartram, Cooper had found, in wilderness, an ample balm to soothe the anguished souls of men—a paradise thought to have been granted us in perpetuity, but which was fated to be annulled by human greed. Already, the overthrow of nature's sovereignty could be seen in Middlesex County and—to Henry's eyes—even in Maine's Piscataquis County, where trees were valued as a commodity.

After Henry and I had been sufficiently rested to continue our search for "mankind's first habitation, where the original dust of creation lay yet upon the doorsill," we set off once more, this time in the company of McCauslin, who had agreed to guide us. An able waterman, as well, he would obtain a vessel farther up the western branch, at Millinocket, which would carry us on the string of spacious lakes that led to Mount Ktaadn.

At the "Burnt Land," we left the road and made our way along the merest sketch of a path following the river's northern bank. Apart from a half a dozen loggers' cabins near the shore, which would stand empty until the river froze, there was not a trace of men or livestock. The loggers would arrive in late fall on the ice-paved Penobscot, fell pines, spruce, yellow birch, fir, mountain ash, and hickories, and—come spring—roll them into the river, which would carry them to Bangor. Before the thaw, most of the men would have traveled the frozen river south, taking their animals. The log drivers would later follow them.

We made camp at the Penobscot's meeting with the Millinocket, the latter more a stream than a river. We had acquired two other skillful boatmen for the better management of our boat, known as a "batteau," a corruption of *bateau*. In its shape, it resembled the French fishing dory, which had been brought to North America during the French and Indian Wars. Unlike a canoe, it had a shallow draft, flared sides, and a narrow stern and bow. By using twelve-foot iron-tipped spruce poles, the boatmen could punt them through the rapids.

By the Millinocket, we drank a wondrous beer favored by the woodsmen of those parts, which Henry, who did not require stimulants to encourage his ecstasies, praised. He extolled its manly virtues in his journal with a J. Thoreau & Co. pencil:

"It was as if we sucked at the very teats of Nature's pine-clad bosom in these parts,—the sap of all Millinocket botany commingled,—the topmost, most fantastic, and spiciest sprays of the primitive wood, and whatever invigorating and stringent gum or essence it afforded steeped and dissolved in it,—a lumberer's drink, which would acclimate and naturalize a man at once,—which would make him see green, and, if he slept, dream that he heard the wind sough among the pines."

While McCauslin and the boatmen dozed at the bottom of our batteau and I rested in the shade of the jack pines, Henry, clearheaded and eager, searched for relics of the Penobscot tribe. He found only stone flakes left from their arrowheads. Seeing him squatting on the dusty ground, like Niobe weeping for her slain children, I joined him in his search.

"The earth's fossil record," he said gloomily, "like arrowheads and pottery shards, the pyramids of the pharaohs, or the skeleton of what had been a moose, in whose bones I found no trace of the muscular animal to which they had once belonged—all point to one end, which is extinction."

He was referring to a bull moose, macerated by wolves and insects into a lathwork of bones, which we had stumbled upon downriver, near Enfield.

He threw his arms wide, as if to embrace what his eyes could take in, and said biblically, "All this will pass into bog meadows and mires, fens and sloughs, where it will be consumed by time. The silver birch trees, the osprey steadying itself above the Penobscot, the river itself with its multitude of fish and water walkers striding across its surface like tiny bateaux will pass, as will also the raucous loons crying over a tragedy known only to loons and the eagles towering above the bastions of Mount Ktaadn, where, according to the Abenaki, the god Pomola, a beast with an eagle's talons and wings, a man's body, and a moose's head, dwells and sends furious storms against the valley's creatures."

He rocked on his heels and pulled at his beard like Jeremiah lamenting the destruction of Jerusalem.

"They will survive for a time in the words I set down in my journals, until the words, too, are destroyed and there is nothing left to tell that this animal or tree, that fish or man had ever been here."

I remember being stricken by Henry's prophesy. I felt

like a limed bird or the fish at the end of a line pulled up into the coruscating light that will finish it. I was glad that McCauslin and the others slept through Henry's forecast of the apocalypse. Stoical and pragmatic—their minds riding upon the rails of the present moment and its dangers—they would have laughed at him. I would not have wished him shamed. By now, I had acknowledged his rarity, though his waywardness would sometimes spoil my good opinion of him.

"Don't be alarmed, Samuel. The end will not come in our time, but in a thousand or ten thousand years hence. Life will take a long time dying. Smell the air, Samuel—how pure it is! There is not an atom of the stench of the dying animal that will someday be ubiquitous until the end has been accomplished."

There was, however, the rancid stink of our buttered boots, which the flies loved!

Henry crouched by the river and drank from his cupped hands.

"Taste the water—how it seems almost to evaporate on the tongue. It is a clear spirit that does not intoxicate—the aqua vitae, supernal water of baptism, even more pristine than our own Walden Pond. Last winter, it was snow falling on cedars in the North Maine Woods. Mark me, Samuel: One day handbills will be given out on the streets of Boston in praise of Hiram Ricker's Poland Spring, and Frederic Tudor's heirs will send blocks of the frozen Penobscot to Calcutta and Charleston."

Henry's mood could be as changeable as the wind; in an instant, it had turned from despondency to rapture. His mind, like a great bird roaming the sky's upper stories, took an effort for him to steady in the sometimes contrary gusts of his thought.

We were then six miles upriver from McCauslin's place and twenty-four from the point, where we ought to have met up with Louis Neptune and his men. We visited the house of Old Fowler, father of one of our boatmen and the oldest inhabitant of those remote woods. His was "the last house" to be seen northwest of Bangor, the lumber town that Henry likened to "a star on the edge of night, still hewing at the forests of which it is built." Henry would pronounce "the last house" with the relish of a man who delights in isolation. In the flattened meadow grass, we saw where moose had lain down to sleep. Old Fowler said that the meadows thereabouts were pasture for thousands of the great beasts, which, in their grotesqueness, seemed almost a thing extant before the Flood.

Our batteau now needed to be carried two miles round the Grand Falls of the Penobscot, the first of our portages as we rowed toward North Twin Lake. Horses were brought up, and the boat put onto a sled made of saplings. Henry and I walked ahead to the falls above the river, near the outlet of Quakish Lake. There, we were surprised by the sight of a pine tree stripped of bark, its sap used to glue a placard to the trunk, announcing to the moose and the Indian the existence of Oak Hall, a haberdashery owned by George W. Simmons, of Boston. Henry raged against the rapacious claw of commerce, while I grew anxious for the existence of an aboriginal world.

"Not all men work with pen and paper," I said—kindly,

to placate him. "Most use the ax, the cleaver, the saw, and the sewing needle, especially here where there is nothing. They *make* things, Henry. . . . The world progresses by fits and starts."

"And by fits and starts, it goes to blazes," he replied in a voice pitched between rancor and sorrow. "And we along with it."

When the batteau arrived, the poor beasts panting after the strain of having hauled it over stony ground, we resumed our journey. There would be other portages before we reached Mount Ktaadn, all of them arduous for the draft horses and for the boatmen, wearing red flannel shirts and waterman's boots, while Henry and I walked ahead in the moccasined footsteps of Indians who had carried birch-bark canoes along these same paths hundreds of years and more ago.

In the journal entries for our expedition, the factual Henry prevailed over the fanciful one. Emerson called them "bare as a lumberman's cabin," although I suspect he had never been inside of one. In his prose Henry commemorated the places and things of the Maine wilderness, as a man would for whom trees, stones, and rivers were enough. He had in mind the "facts of the matter," which, he declared, deserve mention in that what they stand for will one day vanish. A world where all is spirit can no more be understood than an essay on the spirit without the world of things and places to serve as its foil.

"Things cast a shadow called metaphor, which partakes of two worlds at once and is all the richer for it," said Henry.

Just so, do I love to study old maps delineating features

that time has effaced and street directories enumerating residents who long ago departed this world for glory or oblivion. Ghosts of a forgotten world hover above their worn pages; they are the graveyards and gazettes of time—lodestones to which even staunch minds will turn for comfort.

I recall a conversation held between Henry and Emerson. A map of North America lay open on the latter's desk.

"The present state of cartography is, for some of us, more staggering to the mind than the revealed truths of religion."

"Meaning what?" said Henry.

"We know less about the North American continent than we do the nature of God."

Henry the land surveyor snuffled. Emerson rounded off his thought.

"Theologians and clergymen claim to know His will, while every Tom, Dick, and Harry has an opinion about Him. As a result, His ways are no more mysterious than clockwork or the streets and warrens of Boston. But this immensity!" His fingers walked across the empty spaces of the Far West. "None can claim to know it in its entirety."

The Maine wilderness was mystery enough for me. I feared it more than I did God.

Now Henry and I began to see moose where, earlier on our trip, we had seen only their traces in the grass, imprinted on the mud banks, or left to molder down to a collation of imposing bones.

"Moose," Henry said to himself, and then "Indian," as if the words were, to his mind, the poles of a creation little by little falling into ruin.

One night, he dreamed he was fishing from his rustic

bed, near to the river's own. Waking before us while the moon was still up, he tested his nocturnal vision with pole and line—raising, he told us afterward, speckled trout and silvery roach into the moonlight that shone down on the river and on the steep face of Mount Ktaadn, which could be seen now in the distance.

At the Aboljacknagesic, we tied up to a willow tree aslant the creek, and Henry, compass in hand, led us northeastward, toward the mountain's tallest peak. That night, we slept in a deep ravine, keeping ourselves warm—for the air was already chill there—by a fire in which a felled spruce tree was consumed whole. Next morning, Henry went on alone, like a priest ascending to his altar, leaving behind those not ordained to administer the sacraments.

I spent the morning nervously awaiting his return. To pass the time, I practiced my throwing skills—my adroitness with a jackknife having, by this time, become as sharp as the blade itself, so that even the Canuck boatmen marveled at my aim.

WHEN HENRY RETURNED FROM the summit, he did not wish to speak of his experience. He seemed shaken; he brooded, as if seeing in his mind's eye things beyond human ken, which did not bear witnessing. What I know of the hours that he spent on the mountaintop, I would read much later, in a draft of *The Maine Woods*. While I would leave Walden Woods before Henry had given up his experiment and had sought the company of his fellows, we remained friends until his death this year.

To relate the experience that shattered him, I will give voice to his unspoken thoughts—a ventriloquism, in which the roles have been reversed, allowing the puppet to make its master talk.

"On Mount Ktaadn, I was like a man who finds himself suddenly set apart. No . . . I was more like an uncomprehending rock than a man. Hardly even that! A rock is too durable an object to represent a man. I was a stick, then, and liable to be broken—a mere twig snapped in two—by the strength of Titans resident on that mountain peak and in the winds that tore at it, sending the poor sparrows beyond God's providence. I was afraid, very much afraid that I, too, would be cast out, as Satan and his legion had been for their impious revolt, their wings scorched to stumps. I stood in defiance—cowered in dread, to be honest—of a power more puissant than God's and known only to elemental nature and, perhaps, to the ancients who had first appeared in the valleys below and on the pastured slopes of the mountain, where it reigned imperiously as fire does, careless of men and women. The mountain seemed an abandoned quarry, which had been used in the building of the world.

"On Ktaadn, I saw nothing; I had expected to see into the depths of space, but my view was occluded by mist and cloud—more cloud than mist, so that when I drank from the springs there, it seemed I was drinking water wrung from clouds. When the mist briefly lifted its veil, I saw, if you can call it seeing, ancient scenes: Vulcan at his forge, Prometheus upon his rock, and Atlas, the earth upon his shoulders. I was none of them. I was only a man who had blundered arrogantly into a place hostile to all life. And I was afraid.

"I recalled Milton's lines uttered by Satan to the spirits of the abyss: 'Chaos and ancient Night, / I come no spy / With purpose to explore or to disturb / The secrets of your realm . . .'

"As though to affirm my abnegation—my absence—the mist fell around me once again, bandaging my eyes. I myself might have been a cloud, so vague and dissolute did I feel. I was unfinished—the raw clay merely.

"Then the mountain spoke: 'Shouldst thou freeze or starve, or shudder thy life away, here is no shrine, nor altar, nor any access to my ear.'

"I was a little man, who had, in his conceit, held himself aloof from his fellows, believing I had business to transact with potentates. I had traveled smugly in Concord, and now I wished to return there, where nature was not elevated above the common and the lowercase. I had had enough of prodigies.

"I fled the mountain as if it had contained a thousand devils in its granite fastness. I hurried to rejoin my fellows, who instinctually understood that mountains can never belong to men. Nature's monsters should be feared, if the heart is faint, or revered, if it is capable of awe—from the valley, where Flora temperately rules. I hurried to rejoice in my littleness with my companions. Pomola, god of storms and thunder, was sovereign on Mount Ktaadn and more ancient than the Ancient of Days, who must shrink from him."

Such words as those might have passed through Henry's

disconcerted mind. If not those, then some others equally tumultuous.

I, too, had faced a "true source of evil"; mine had been near Carrollton, Isle of White County, Virginia, where Nature wore her malignancy beneath her pretty skirts. There evil had not been in mountains, but in men. In slavery's inferno, I had been stewed to pulp. Each whip stroke had been an apocalypse. So I might not have presumed too much in speaking for Henry.

He had come down from the mountaintop with neither tablets of the law nor the voice of God resounding in his ear. His hair and beard had not turned white. He had not been touched by fire, but by ice and Nature's cold, mineral heart. Glory did not cover him; he frowned and kept his thoughts to himself.

We started back to Bangor.

Later, as if to mock Henry and his ideas of the wilderness, we finally met up with Louis Neptune and his men, sitting slumped in their canoes, on the Millinocket.

"Me been sick," Louis moaned, his wizened, nut brown face resting in his hands. "Oh, me unwell now."

The Indians had been detained by too much Bangor whiskey, downriver at Five Islands, where boatmen and loggers caroused. They had exchanged their rags for the caped overcoats and wide-brimmed hats favored by Quakers. They were as far removed from the state of nature as were the frightened muskrats scuffling at the bottom of the canoes, destined to be roasted and eaten during the trip to Chesuncook Lake, where the Indians intended to hunt for moose. They looked outlandish in their somber clothes, which became them even less than had their rags.

"They ought to have visited Oak Hall," said Henry wryly. "Mr. Simmons, of Boston, could have turned them into gents."

I smiled, gladdened by Henry's good humor, which the world outside Walden could sometimes darken, but was a welcome accent, an ornament in a somber hymn.

"Me sure get some moose!" boasted Louis Neptune.

Henry turned his back on him—a slight the Indian did not acknowledge.

The Indians continued up Millinocket Stream, where they vanished into time's maw, where truths are turned into myths, myths receive their tarnish, and the primordial world is rubbished.

"Game of mumblety-peg?" asked Henry, opening his jackknife.

We played like two boys whose ambition was the mastery of simple skills and whose summits were no grander than Brister's Hill.

Ktaadn and Pomola might be briefly endured, but they would never offer rest or inspire reverence in our kind. Theirs was a brutal nature to be feared. Henry would sometimes feel the itch to travel beyond Concord once again, but not in search of transfiguration that would merge him with the atoms of creation. The sense of dissolution had been too terrible to bear repeating.

We reached Bangor on September 10—the day the Donner Party finished its agonizing crawl across the Great Salt Lake Desert. Nature is as indifferent and willful as a locomotive, which would as soon crush a child beneath its wheels as a dog.

ON A NIGHT NOT LONG AFTER OUR RETURN to Walden, Henry invoked nature's genial spirit. He paddled his canoe out onto the pond and—letting it come to rest, in accord with Newton's laws of motion—looked once again at the luminous figures traced against the sky. They told familiar stories of the classical age. Stars were thickly sown on the black sky and on the blacker surface of the pond. He was, Henry later said, like an aeronaut who watches one vista yield to the next in the grand and endless recessional of space.

"My place is here among the woodland gods. Henceforth, I'll be like the shepherd in a pastoral who summers in the uplands with his flock and, when the pockets of the clouds begin to fill with snow and hailstones, winters in the village with men like himself."

I would not have called Henry a changed man. He did not go up the mountain only to come down as someone else. He was humbled, not transformed. No longer content to play the part of the outcast, he took up—though not completely, for he would always be an eccentric and a dreamer—the business of mankind and managed to transact it in a way that did not diminish himself in his own eyes. Like other men, he was afraid to die alone—to speak his last words into the unhearing night, which might usher in eternity or extinction. The dying and the fear of it come to us all, even to a New England Transcendentalist.

That night on Walden Pond, Henry came out from under the stars.

And what about Samuel Long? What became of him after having stood in the shadow of Mount Ktaadn? He had traveled as far north as he needed. He was no freer—no less liable to be seized, chained up, and hurried into bondage once again and, very possibly, death. But he had come to realize that his woeful condition was that of every man and that there was no last stop on the Underground Railroad. There could be no safe haven. This realization did not cause him to forgive his tormentors or pity them their ignorance or to fear them less. He became warier than before, hard, and a little deceitful. He worried the splinter in his heart, partly in anxiousness, partly for the strange pleasure he took in it, like wriggling a loose tooth in the gum. He became jealous of his own life and determined to hold it fast with the one good hand that was left to him.

Philadelphia, Pennsylvania
December 20, 1862

I had thought to end my story of Henry David Thoreau here. I would stay on awhile longer in Concord, but my days with him in Walden Woods were over, though our friendship would be renewed, at intervals, until his death. Emerson was as good as his word. He arranged for my manumission, and, in the spring

of 1847, I became a freedman; in the fall of 1848, I entered Middlebury College, in Vermont.

Having been graduated in due course by that enlightened institution, I went to work for William Garrison, at The Liberator, *in Boston, where I took up residence in December 1851. I was employed in various capacities, including that of correspondent. In April 1864, I removed to Philadelphia, where I continued my profession at* The Christian Recorder. *After Mr. Lincoln's Emancipation Proclamation, the columns of that paper could scarcely contain the fire that, for two centuries, had been no more than an ember in the hearts of my people.*

In June, the Recorder's *editor, Elisha Weaver, sent me to Washington City, where I was to make the acquaintance of Walt Whitman, poet of* Leaves of Grass *and a nurse at the Armory Square Hospital, located in the city. As one who had borne witness to the years of sorrow and slaughter—the chief accountant of their losses—we wanted his testimony concerning them; we wanted a précis in prose or verse to grace the pages of our newspaper.*

Not even Whitman, I thought as I looked for him among the wounded, could summarize so complex and multifarious a tragedy. He would need to be Homer in order to write our Iliad. *Perhaps he was, but I did not think so at the time.*

During the two days I spent in conversation with Whitman, I became increasingly sure of his benevolence, and, on my last night in Washington City, I told him the story recounted in the preceding pages. Encouraged by his frankness and his earnestness, I confided in him—albeit hesitantly—an incident that had followed Henry's and my return to Concord after the expedition to Mount Ktaadn. I could see that my disclosure had shaken the good man. He was silent for a time afterward.

"Why did you tell me this?" he finally asked.

His tone was more puzzled than censorious. It was as though I had given him an object that had no apparent use or meaning, to which gift he had responded, "What am I to make of it?"

"I don't know," I said honestly, for I did not know. "Forget that I ever spoke of it."

"A thing once said cannot be unsaid."

I looked out the window of his room at a sky that appeared suddenly alien. I might have been on Mars for all I knew of earth at that moment.

"I must think about what you've told me." My face, even by candlelight, must have betrayed my unease, for he said, "Never fear that I will betray you, Samuel."

We shook hands, and I never saw him again, although I have read his book many times since. The week following my return to Philadelphia, I received this letter:

*468 M. Street, South
Washington City*

July 4, 1864

Dear Mr. Long,

Publish your reminiscence, if you must, but I entreat you to suppress its "final chapter," for the sake of Henry Thoreau's reputation, as well as your own safety. You will not escape peril until you, like him, are beyond the reach of little men. I am afraid, Samuel, that most men are pygmies.

Sincerely,

Walt Whitman

I had no wish to see my memoir published. I scarcely know why I had troubled to write it. Having become, at last, a freedman, I wished nothing more than to spend the balance of my days as a private one. Nonetheless, I finished the story, adding a last chapter. I intend to put the manuscript away among my papers and souvenirs. Perhaps a descendant, if I ever marry; a legal heir, if I have property to convey or business left undone; or some stranger who happens on it will decide otherwise than I have and send it to a publisher. I leave the matter in other, future hands.

VII

hile Henry sat in his canoe on Walden Pond, admiring the stars and preparing to make himself adaptable to the ordinary ways of men, I was sitting at my table, cutting an apple with my knife. I was tired, having spent much of the day at Bush, helping the Emersons "put away the garden" for another year. Now at home in my cabin, I gave myself luxuriously to the sensations of the body's easing the spring of its mechanism, which had been tightly wound by toil.

Darkness had risen like a flood of black water. I sat eating the apple in a circle of candlelight. I was content, as a man can be taking his ease in his own house, especially at night, when his eyes are untroubled by shabbiness.

"Each must build up his own world," Emerson had once said to me, "though he unbuilt all other men's, for materials."

I had not heard the footsteps in the dooryard nor on the step outside the door. I was too intent on my own thoughts. Suddenly, the door gave way with a noise of splintering wood. A man stood in the doorway, a black hulk against the starlit night behind him.

For an instant, I thought Carlson, father of the drowned boy, had returned.

"Well, nigger," the man said, stepping across the threshold. "You been telling tales. Tall ones!" He tossed a copy of *The Liberator* on the table. By the light of the candle, I saw that it was the issue in which my narrative had appeared. "Your bellyaching has done for you. Your old master sent me to fetch you. He wants to hear from your own nigger lips how he hurt your feelings and all. He wants to make amends. He got a room ready and waiting for you. Cozy little room with a blanket and a pillow to rest your nappy head on. Pretty soon, you going to be in hog heaven."

He had a pistol in his hand, which he now cocked and aimed at me.

"Get up, boy! Time to be going."

I had not said a word, nor had I taken my eyes off him. Suddenly, I blew out the candle and leaned away from the path of the bullet. He fired blindly into the darkness. My small room was filled with the stink of gunpowder. The man hunter coughed. I took my knife and threw it at the black shape he made in the doorway. The knife stuck in his throat. He fell to the floor, a hand pressed to his neck, blood oozing between the fingers. With hardly a thought, I plucked out the knife and finished him.

I do not know how long I sat on the floor, next to the man hunter's corpse, my eyes watering in the acrid smoke. I was neither jubilant nor remorseful. Gradually, the smoke drifted out the doorway like a ghost. I remember hearing a night bird calling in the woods. I remember the sound of scampering paws beneath the cabin floor. I heard the echo of the pistol shot, but it was only in my mind that I heard it.

I was satisfied. Slowly, however, I realized that, if found out, I would most likely be hanged in the yard outside Middlesex County jail, where Henry had luxuriated in the delicious sensations of rebelliousness.

I had killed a white man, never mind that he had forced my door and drawn his pistol on me. I could picture the trial—the eloquent pleadings of Henry, Emerson, Hawthorne, Garrison, the gruff kindness of Sam Staples, Lidian's tears. . . . But they would plead and weep in vain. The law would take its arctic course and have its way with me.

I went to Henry's cabin, but he was not at home. I thought of the pond and went there. I could see him on the water in his canoe. He was paddling toward shore. I waited for him on the beach.

"Samuel," he said, too loudly for my unstrung nerves.

I hushed him.

"What is it, Samuel?" He shone his lantern on my face. "You look ghastly in this light."

"I just killed a man hunter," I said without preamble.

He hurried to my cabin, lighting our way with the lantern. With it, he examined my handiwork lying crumpled on the floor.

"Not a pretty sight," he said, stroking his beard.

I laughed nervously. My knees felt unhinged. I sat down on the chair.

"This is a bad business, Samuel."

"I don't know what to do," I muttered.

"He has to be gotten rid of."

His matter-of-factness took me by surprise. I took heart.

"I thought maybe we could plant him in the bean field."

"To increase the harvest," he said wryly. "It would be the only good thing he'd ever do in this world."

"Shall I get the barrow?" I asked. My voice was strained by the contrary impulses of eagerness and despondency.

He nodded. I wheeled the barrow from behind the cabin to the front door, and, together, we manhandled the body into it.

"Just like wrestling a bag of feed," said Henry.

I laughed nervously again.

We started toward the bean field, the barrow jolting over ruts and rocks. Henry stopped abruptly and let go of the wooden handles.

"Bean field won't serve," he said tersely. "Animals'll dig him up. Then some poor soul looking to appease his hunger with my crop will stumble over him. I couldn't sleep nights for worrying about it."

"What shall we do, then?" I asked anxiously.

I felt the warmth of the rising sun on me, but it was only the heat of exertion. The night still held sway and concealed my crime. Even now, I call it a crime, though I do not believe it. We are creatures of the law—even the lawless, who scoff at it and, for its sake, live in fear of discovery and then, to satisfy it, die by a bullet or a noose.

"We'll put him in the pond," said Henry decisively. "Wait here."

He left and, in a short while, returned with a chain used to clear the fields of stumps. I pushed the barrow with its deadweight toward the water. We went in stealth, afraid to light the lamp. My heart worked like a bellows. Henry kept silent.

We dumped the body onto the sand. While I shifted it, Henry wound the heavy chain about it, which he secured with a padlock, so that the body could not be raised by the action of the currents or the effect of decomposition into the light of day, where justice is served. I say "justice," for form's sake. I tell you that I felt no contrition and feel none now.

We carried the body, made ponderous by the addition of the chain, to the canoe, and then we paddled onto the lake. It might have been an ocean, so very small we seemed under night's immensity. I could not see the shore or the trees beyond it; my mind was taken up—beset by distractions of its own making.

We seem to stir the stars each time we dip our paddles into the pond, I said to myself.

I was proud to have coined so clever a figure. I almost repeated it to Henry, but I was reminded of our dread purpose when my naked foot touched the dead man's.

Henry's fancy also seemed to be preternaturally active, for he quoted from *Paradise Lost*. He did so in a whisper, suitable for so awesome and dangerous an occasion as ours.

> ". . . Him the Almighty Power
> Hurld headlong flaming from th' Ethereal Skie
> With hideous ruine and combustion down
> To bottomless perdition, there to dwell
> In Adamantine Chains and penal Fire."

"I suppose to liken a man hunter to the author of all evil is extravagant. . . . Or maybe not. I leave it to you to decide, Samuel, as well as the scouring of your bloody cabin floor."

I kept my thoughts to myself.

Henry had steered us to the pond's deepest place, seventeen fathoms, midway between "Thoreau's Cove" and Little Cove. We pulled the body over the side and nearly swamped the boat in doing it.

"He will not trouble you again, Samuel."

I thanked him with as much fervor as my shaken spirit could muster.

We turned the canoe about and paddled across to "Thoreau's Cove." Stars no longer shone upon the water—their fiery particles had been put out. I could not help feeling all of Concord's eyes on me. I could not see Henry's. I would never know how much, if anything, it had cost him to become my accomplice.

"Next winter, when the ice returns and, with it, Mr. Tudor's men, Walden Pond will have lost its purity," he said. Whether he had spoken ironically or sadly, I could not judge.

We never spoke of that night again.

Philadelphia, Pennsylvania
July 17, 1864

"Moose . . . Indian."

—Thoreau's last words, May 6, 1862,
overheard by William Ellery Channing

Acknowledgments

I DO NOT CLAIM TO BE A HISTORIAN, however much this story will be seen to rise from history's particulars. Like any other novelist of the kind, my fiction appropriates the past—its people, places, organizations, political debate, wars, and chronology—in the interest of storytelling. I need only ask the specialists of the time to recall that Thoreau shaped his and his brother's two-week-long boat trip to Plymouth, New Hampshire, and back to Walden Pond, when writing *A Week on the Concord and Merrimack Rivers*. I have taken occasional liberties with the sequence of events. (I might have blamed them on Samuel Long's faulty memory.)

To have written this story from a first-person viewpoint that claims to belong to a black man and a slave is a presumption; my motives were the highest, among them to learn something new about myself and to reflect on Samuel Long's ordeals as a member of the race responsible for them. (Whether or not the responsibility continues even unto the present day, I leave to the readers' consciences.) In any case, no sooner has a writer set words to paper than he or she has presumed, but unless one is willing to appropriate the lives of others—fictional or factual—to achieve an honorable end, the writing cannot escape the gravity of the authorial self. I did intend that this book should have an honorable aim, whether or not it succeeds in achieving it.

I have relied on a number of works by Thoreau, Emerson, and Hawthorne, but I have also read or consulted invaluable secondary sources: *The Adventures of Henry Thoreau: A Young Man's Unlikely Path to Walden Pond*, by Michael Sims; *Emerson Among the Eccentrics: A Group Portrait*, by Carlos Baker; *Henry David Thoreau*, by Frank B. Sanborn; *Narrative of the Life and Adventures of Henry Bibb, An American Slave, Written by Himself*; *Narrative of the Life of Frederick Douglass, An American Slave, Written by Himself*; as well as *Born in Slavery: Slave Narratives from the Federal Writers' Project, 1936–1938*. Some of the lines spoken by Thoreau, Emerson, and Hawthorne were in fact theirs; most, however, have been given to them without, I hope, giving them cause to regret my imposition.

I acknowledge my debt, once again and with pleasure, to Bellevue Literary Press, to my publisher, Erika Goldman, to the press's founding publisher, Jerome Lowenstein, M.D., and to Leslie Hodgkins, Crystal Sikma, Molly Mikolowski, Joe Gannon, and Carol Edwards, as well as to Eugene Lim, novelist and friend, for his many kindnesses. My gratitude to Helen, my wife, is one of my life's constants.

ABOUT THE AUTHOR

NORMAN LOCK is the award-winning author of novels, short fiction, and poetry, as well as stage, radio, and screenplays. His most recent books are the short story collection *Love Among the Particles*, a *Shelf Awareness* Best Book of the Year, and three previous books in The American Novels series: *The Boy in His Winter*, a reenvisioning of Mark Twain's classic *The Adventures of Huckleberry Finn*, which Scott Simon of NPR *Weekend Edition* said, "make[s] Huck and Jim so real you expect to get messages from them on your iPhone"; *American Meteor,* an homage to Walt Whitman and William Henry Jackson named a Firecracker Award finalist and *Publishers Weekly* Best Book of the Year; and *The Port-Wine Stain*, a "mesmerizingly twisted, richly layered" (*New York Times Book Review*) homage to Edgar Allan Poe and Thomas Dent Mütter.

Lock has won The Dactyl Foundation Literary Fiction Award, *The Paris Review* Aga Khan Prize for Fiction, and writing fellowships from the New Jersey State Council on the Arts, the Pennsylvania Council on the Arts, and the National Endowment for the Arts. He lives in Aberdeen, New Jersey, where he is at work on the next books of The American Novels series.

BELLEVUE LITERARY PRESS is devoted to publishing
literary fiction and nonfiction at the intersection of
the arts and sciences because we believe that science and the
humanities are natural companions for understanding the
human experience. With each book we publish, our goal is
to foster a rich, interdisciplinary dialogue that will forge new
tools for thinking and engaging with the world.

To support our press and its mission, and for our full catalogue
of published titles, please visit us at blpress.org.

BELLEVUE LITERARY PRESS

New York